What people are saying about

I NEVER DO THIS

"Narrated with a noirish sensibility, the novel follows a 27-year-old woman named LaDene Faye Howell as she recounts the tale of how and why she's currently in police custody. LaDene's narration is full of personality and flair. Miller has crafted a compelling cast of characters, from LaDene's churchgoing family to her fellow pregnant classmates at New Dawn Ministry to the overbearing faculty who ruthlessly rule the school. Even the humorous description of the crimes she committed with Bobby is rendered in engaging detail. Everyone from casual readers to the staunchest of mystery fans will find something to enjoy in this quick—and quick-witted—read."

—*Kirkus Reviews*

* * *

"Loved it. Miller has written a masterful novel, inhabited by a voice so fearless and compassionate, urgent and heartland-true, that its music and message stay with you long, long after the final page. Indeed, *I Never Do This* is one of those rare books that makes you want to read it all over again, so compelling and beautifully limned are the characters."

—Brandon R. Schrand, author of *The Enders Hotel*, *Works Cited*, and *Psychiana Man*

"Haunting. Feels like an ultra-personal conversation. Grabs you immediately and refuses to let go."

—Peter Edwards, *The Toronto Star*, co-author of *The Wolfpack: The Millennial Mobsters who Brought Chaos and the Cartels to the Canadian Underworld*, with Luis Horacio Najera

* * *

"I'm blown away by Anesa Miller's beautiful writing. She's definitely a master storyteller! Miller leads the reader so deftly down the trail of her protagonist's past that I became consumed by this mesmerizing story. I loved the book."

—Kathy Wollenberg, author of *Far Less*

* * *

"LaDene's voice propels us as she recounts her life of family dysfunction, religious fundamentalism, abuse, and how we can't escape the darker impulses of family even when we think we've broken from them. As her story unfolds, we witness how fast a person's life can unravel from a chance encounter. What I love is that the book starts with the confession of a crime, and suspense lies in how the heroine ended up there. For me, this makes it more compelling than the classic mystery or thriller. This suspense holds us to the end we thought we saw coming, but didn't."

—Jerry D. Mathes II, author of *Shipwrecks and Other Stories* and *Ahead of the Flaming Front: A Life on Fire*

"LaDene Howell, the vibrant, colorful narrator of Anesa Miller's marvelous novel, *I Never Do This,* has not lived an easy life. She is a survivor, thick-skinned, full of pain, yet soldiers on. Raised in a harsh, religious family, she is sent away as a teenager when an unintended pregnancy is seen as both something to be punished for and a chance at redemption. After giving her child up for adoption, she earns her GED and then a nursing credential. She supports herself, lives her life, harms no one, and is harmed by no one. That is, until her cousin, Bobby Frank, pays her a visit. Bobby has addiction issues and is full of simmering rage. His presence loosens something in LaDene, and she opens up to him. What starts out as a harmless afternoon spent outdoors and having a few drinks turns sinister when Bobby spots someone from their past and decides a long-overdue confrontation is in order. Set in Ohio and Missouri, America's Midwest comes alive in Miller's pages. Coupled with LaDene's path from child to woman to criminal, *I Never Do This* is a first-rate novel from an insightful and talented author."

—Anne Leigh Parrish, author of *A Summer Morning*

* * *

"Anesa Miller's *I Never Do This* is a gritty novel with a gritty young heroine who must find a way to save herself from those who would save her from herself. I read it in one sitting."

—Mary Clearman Blew, author of *Think of Horses*

Praise for *Our Orbit*

"*Our Orbit* explores how family can be torn apart by brutal conviction and brought together by moments of grace. Anesa Miller writes with wisdom about our need to believe, our desire to belong, and, finally, the best that our fallen world can offer: love, forgiveness, a chance to start over again."

—Kim Barnes, Author of *In the Kingdom of Men*

* * *

"Deftly woven, complex and compelling. Memorable characters hold the reader's attention from beginning to end."

— *The Midwest Book Review*

* * *

"Rejecting simplistic stereotypes, Miller invites readers to probe beyond immediate impressions. A compassionate, thoughtful narrative about hard-won self-realizations."

— Kirkus Reviews

I
NEVER
DO
THIS

A Novel

ANESA MILLER

Sibylline Press

AN IMPRINT OF ALL THINGS BOOK

Sibylline Press
Copyright © 2024 Anesa Miller
All Rights Reserved.

Published in the United States by Sibylline Press,
an imprint of All Things Book LLC, California.
Sibylline Press is dedicated to publishing the brilliant work of
women authors ages 50 and older.
www.sibyllinepress.com

Distributed to the trade by Publishers Group West.
Sibylline Press
Paperback ISBN: 9781960573988
eBook ISBN: 9781960573087
Library of Congress Control Number: 2023947612

Book and Cover Design: Alicia Feltman

Permissions:
Page 151 - Poem "The Fairies" by William Allington.
Page 168 - "Dreamland" is a traditional Cajun lullaby.

I
NEVER
DO
THIS

A Novel

VANESA MILLER

Part I

I, LaDene Faye Howell, will recount the events of August 12, 2019, including all relevant background leading up to the encounter that I understand you are investigating. I will tell all in full truth and will hold nothing back to protect myself from the eyes of the law. Other persons involved do not know the full history of how and why things took place as they did. I'm the only one who can tell it all.

I am the person who cut Mr. Jonathan Rutherford with a ten-inch folding knife, approximately. I made two cuts to his face, or rather the forehead—just about one inch long each, with the sharp edge of the blade tip. Also one cut on his chest. Very shallow cuts. In doing this, I acted alone. In fact, I meant to keep the exact nature of my actions secret. I told Mr. Rutherford to play dead. He may have been screaming when I said it. He did scream at one point, as I recollect. But I feel certain he heard me. I bent right to his ear.

"Act like you're dyin'," I told him.

He had been talking too much in general over the whole evening. I tried many times to quiet him down for his own good. I tried to do this in a nice way. A calm way. But once I took the knife, I finally got his attention. He will surely testify to that. I said it would all be for show.

No. I never stabbed, struck, nor slapped or kicked Mr. Rutherford in any way. I did not strike him with my hand, knee, or any object. It is possible he was struck by another person. He may have been shoved or otherwise roughed up in a minor sort of way. I don't know all details of that to a certainty, but I did not witness any physical beating being done to him.

For most of the evening, Mr. Rutherford appeared to co-operate willingly with all that was happening. He was offered food and drink over a period of three to four hours. Yes, I my-self gave him snacks and cold tea. No, I never heard him say flat-out, "You folks just let me go, now." He did not say that. He was free to talk and dispute, which he did. Like I say, he talked more than was probably wise on his part. Yes, from his viewpoint, he probably felt he was subjected to harassment. Maybe even intimidation. I expect he did feel that way.

Let's just get it down on your recording right now that this man you keep calling my "confederate" is Robert Franklin Howell. He is known to most as Bobby Frank. The knife be-longs to him, that's correct. He "produced" the knife at an earlier point in the evening. From his pants pocket, I guess, but I didn't see for sure at the time. Absolutely not—Bobby Frank did not cut anyone. Not in my presence. Not last night, nor at any time in our past history that I have ever observed.

Bobby Frank is a relation to me. I've known him all my life. He's a second cousin by a different mother—what some people call middling kin. We've always been friendly. No, we are not "intimate partners" and never have been.

I'm aware that you are empowered to lie to me, but don't bother saying that Bobby Frank pinned something on me. Like it was my revenge, snatching the old man, or I had a dire plan from the git-go, or any other shit on that line. He's not about to say that. And I won't be pinning stuff on him that he didn't do, neither. I will only speak what really happened. I pledged to that already.

I am 27 years of age. Bobby Frank is about nine years older than me, so that would make him 35 or 36, I guess. I don't know where he's been residing lately. He may not have a proper address. It looked like he'd been more or less camping in the house on Duck Creek Road—that house where the incident with Mr. Rutherford took place.

That house used to be in our family. It was our Gramma Dot's place. I don't know who owns it now.

You are aware that I sent my sister to check on the old man, right? When we left him at that house, I stopped and called her. Told her to go over right away and see to his welfare. How he was holding up after what happened.

Mr. Rutherford was the principal of Marietta High School for many years. He was in charge when Bobby Frank attended there, and he was still principal later on when I came up. That's how we knew him, from back when. No, categorically *not*— we never stalked him, never surveilled him, nothing like that. It was a pure stroke of fate that he happened to exit the Speedway on State Route 60 precisely when he did. Me and Bobby were driving north at that moment. It was me who recognized him. Well, that only makes sense, don't it? It's been, like, 20 years since Bobby was in school. Only about ten years for me.

Okay, twelve years, to be exact.

Bobby said, "Who's that old coot coming out the Speedway?"

Well, I didn't know for certain, but I said, "Looks like old Mr. Rutherford."

Yes, me and Bobby both had our episodes back in school days.

No, we did not leave Mr. Rutherford at the old house "to die." Absolutely not. I am an LPN. I knew very well he wasn't cut up to where he would bleed out. Nowhere close. Didn't he state what I whispered to him? I told him, "Just *play* dead."

You don't believe I'm going to tell you everything? Buckle up, Bud. You will hear all. Every ray of truth scatters the darkness. So help me God.

* * *

HOW WOULD I DESCRIBE MYSELF? You're looking right at me. I'm your typical small-town, youngish, white woman.

Oh, all right, then. I am five foot four inches tall. I weigh about 145, last I checked. Everybody in my family has these same green eyes and freckles. This is my natural hair color—your basic light brown. I wear a fishtail braid most days, that's why it appears wavy. At home, I leave it loose like this.

Thank you. At work they call me Rapunzel because I can sit on my braid.

I was always known as a quiet girl. I'm still quiet, mostly. I was a decent student, probably had about a B-plus average. Stopped going to school at fifteen, finished online. Took the GED when I was seventeen. I work a steady job at Riverside Senior Care on White Hill Road. Split shifts. I live in the Haven House Apartment Building on the southwest side of Marietta. Been there eight years now. I've got a ground-level place with the little fenced patio.

One bedroom. No kids. Never married.

Happy now?

If you're familiar with Washington County, you'll know that the Howell family has been here forever. Our first Ohio ancestor had a land grant on a west bend of the Muskingum River. That was payment for fighting the Revolutionary War. (My sister Jo Beth even joined the DAR.) We figure our ancestor got sick of his crops washing out in every spring flood. So he looked around for a less susceptible line of work and established the first ferry crossing in the territory. It was what's called a cable-type ferry, run on homemade rope "thick as a strong man's arm," so the story goes. They say you had to wheel that cable up on bear grease. Later they upgraded to iron chains and pulleys, anchored to the fattest trees of the old-growth forest. That ferry brought a good livelihood for quite some time.

Too bad for us descendants—cable ferries did not become a wave of the future. Dams got built, locks got dug. Bridges. Railway. Gramma said when she was a girl, elder folks were still moaning about the ferry shutting down for good. "We shoulda been millionaires!" and remarks to that effect.

Boo-hoo.

Another open secret: There's two branches to the Howells of southern Ohio. Been that way for generations. My side is called Fannette's line, in honor of our dad's twice-great grandpa's first wife, Fannette. She planted plum trees on their farm east of Coal Run, and she had half a dozen babies. After that, she could do no more—gave up this life at a youngish age, about 48, with several grandbabies already coming along.

Well, that great-grandpa who was married to Fannette decided he needed a second family after she passed. (His name was Elis Howell, same as my father's name. Men's names tend to repeat a lot. Maybe you've noticed.) So after Fannette, Old Great-Grandpa Elis Howell proceeded to marry a young woman named Maybeth Twist. She gave him another series of kids. I don't even know how many. Now, Maybeth may have been an upstanding woman—my side never delved much into her historic details—but her youngest boy, a Robert Evan, started the outlaw streak of what came to be called "the Twist line." Or some call them the Twist-Howells.

You see, motherless though they were, Fannette's kids had certain advantages. She came from prosperous people. They owned a button factory, and all Fannette's boys got work there. At least seasonal work. My father's own grandpa ran a mussel-fishing crew up and down the Muskingum. Old-timers harked back to it with loads of pride. They harvested great heaps of mussel shell, which the factory turned into pretty buttons of all sizes. Our Gramma Dot still had a little collection of shell buttons from the factory. Kept them in a pimento jar next to her sugar bowl on the hutch shelf.

But then along came the Great Depression. I suppose it's a law of Nature: Hard times hit, fancy buttons go out the window. And plastic was taking over about then, anyways.

Point is, when the factory went belly up, the Howells on Fannette's line still had some cushion to fall on. A little education, or something to sell. Still today, our people are dairymen, EMTs, orderlies, and decorated veterans. Meanwhile, the Twist line turned out black sheep. The younger Robert Evan drove a truck for a bootlegger. Everybody did some moonshinin' in the day, but this was a big ol' gangster operation. When Robert went up to the Mansfield Reformatory, he left a huddled mass of hungry kids behind.

One of those kids grew up to be my father's old friend Robert Franklin. We call him Uncle Bobby. Other people call him Big Bobby. He is the father of Bobby Frank, my well-removed cousin that I'm telling you about.

To wrap all that up—the Twist Howells have shown over the years that they are not picky when it comes to putting food on the table. Honest work is not required. Scale-tipping, tax-dodging, all kinds of scamming, gambling—that's what they get up to. And by all accounts, they're not one bit ashamed of it.

We used to see quite a bit of Uncle Bobby and all the relations. Howells from three counties would clan up for Christmas, Fourth of July, and major birthdays, three-four times a year. Summers, when I was little, a bunch of us would gather at Gramma Dot's place there by the creek. That stretch tends to flood nowadays, but there used to be a nice meadow where the dads would set up picnic tables—ten tables or more, all across the grass. "Every kind of victuals you ever did see," like that old song. There'd be dozens of kids, all running wild. Wade, climb, swing, tag, hide'n'seek. You name it.

Must have been one of those get-togethers, I first got to know Bobby Frank. Of course, he ran with the big kids, being that much older than me. Still, from my earliest memory he was one of the nicer cousins. Used to give us little ones piggyback rides, rolled us around in the wheelbarrow and such. Stuff like that means a lot to smaller children in the middle of a family mob scene.

No, I ain't forgot—I *am* telling you what happened with Mr. Rutherford. Didn't you say you wanted to hear every detail and all the "motives"? That's exactly what I'm getting to.

Now, I was born in the days of President Bill Clinton. I am the baby of my family, youngest of four. I have two sisters, both living in Washington County, and one brother, deceased. Mason fell with the first American soldiers to die in Afghanistan. Nineteen years old. It feels like I barely knew my brother. But him dying divided my childhood in half.

I had started third grade. It was early fall, still hot weather. Right before lunchtime, Momma came and took me out of class. She did not explain what had happened. I didn't fully catch onto the situation till later, not till evening. Or maybe not even till the funeral. All I knew was, Momma brought me home and had me put on my dark-blue church dress and good shoes. But instead of going out somewhere in those nice clothes, we went upstairs in our own house.

First, I waited in the doorway of my parents' room while Momma took a nice fabric-covered box from the lower shelf of her nightstand. I had seen that box before, but only learned just then that it contained the postcards and letters my brother had sent home since he joined the Marines. We took that box into Mason's room, across the hall, and Momma had me sit down at his little wooden desk. She told me to arrange all those mailings in order, from the oldest to most recent.

Momma sounded pretty calm when she showed me how to find a postmark if there was no date in Mason's handwriting. She wanted the cards without envelopes organized separately. But once she left me to tackle that chore, her feelings took free rein. First, she stood at the window and started to gasp for air. Then she went real quiet for a minute before she started singing little snatches of a tune. "Love Makes the World Go Round," I believe it was. A few times, she moaned Mason's name. I didn't understand what was wrong. She paced from his shelves to his dresser, then to the closet. Flipped through his clothes, took out a few shirts, and left them on the bed, like she forgot what she'd started. Then she turned to picking up his baseball things, his trophies, and his action figure collection. She rearranged everything, like a display.

Every so often, she'd come over to me, bend down by the chair and grab me into her arms. For a while then, she sobbed out loud. I patted her shoulder, but when I asked what was the matter, she shook her head real fast, and I could tell she didn't want to talk about it.

My aunties began showing up downstairs. When they tried to talk to Momma, she said things like, "Let me be. I need to get organized here." She shut the bedroom door and started pacing all over again.

Somebody brought my sisters home from the middle school. They also got dressed up and came to sit on Mason's bed. They joined in Momma's crying, but I remember thinking, they were faking it. Like, they made a lot of noise, but their eyes only got red from rubbing, and their faces stayed dry. Or maybe I had those thoughts because I just didn't get it. Maybe the big girls were as confused as me. The concept of getting "killed in the war" had not been much talked about yet in those days. I remember, when Jo Beth whispered to me, it sounded like some notion from a book.

You could tell when my father came home, because the noise level downstairs rose considerably. The backdoor had got locked by mistake, or for whatever reason, and he wound up breaking out the glass to get it open. I can't say if he was in a rage of grief or frustration or what. It got kind of frightening. The relations tried to calm him down, but he stormed upstairs to where we were, banged open the door, and grabbed Momma by her upper arms.

He shouted, "*What* did they say?" and "What do they know for *sure?*" Lots of different outbursts like that.

At last, we girls shed some real tears.

After that, our aunties took us down to sit in the living room. They distracted us by asking questions. When did we last hear from Mason? Was he a specialist? Where did he train? I knew some of those answers from the letters. Out in the kitchen, I could see the countertops filling with food, and I wondered when we would get to eat.

Once the house was crowded enough, I snuck a few cookies and went to my hidey-hole: the girls' room closet. I spent lots of time there in my growing years. No, I do not mean sexual orientation. It was an ordinary bedroom closet, and it was my special place where I could play and keep to myself. For years, I slept in there most nights.

The girls' room—our room—was on the first floor of the house. That's because Momma kept having daughters, and the upstairs bedrooms were smaller, which made it hard for three to share. Since I was the youngest and never quite part of my big sisters' team, so to say, I felt cozier in my little separate closet-place. I had my china animals on a wooden box in there, and I could sing with no one telling me off most of the time. Momma was okay with the set-up. She helped me make a "pallet-bed," like she called it—a couple of yoga mats and an old flannel sleeping bag. In high school, when Jo Beth got work at the Stage store downtown and had her own money, she bought a clothes rack that her and Effie set up as a divider in the middle of the bedroom.

"So LD won't be underfoot all the time." I remember Jo Beth saying that.

It's what they called me at home back then—LD. As a nickname, I never cared for it, but I didn't get much say.

Even after Mason was gone, none of us got to claim his room. Effie was the eldest and boldest, so no doubt she would of tried, except for what happened a month or so after the funeral.

Once it started to sink in that Mason would not be coming home, and once my parents started to accept that hard fact as a permanent fact of life, many things changed in our family.

My sisters are one year apart, and they are alike in lots of ways. Effie is five years ahead of me, and Jo Beth, four. Not long after Mason got killed, Effie changed her name from what we used to call her. Up till then, we called her Rosie, which was short for her real name of Rosephanie, after our momma's favorite aunt. On every occasion, our Momma would holler, "Rosephanie, get over here," and "Rosephanie, clear up this mess," or whatnot. Momma was the only one to use that full, long name.

Rosie (soon to become Effie) was known for pilfering little things around the house, or even out on visits—coins, cupboard snacks, cigarettes. She would empty a whole candy dish into her pockets. Momma combatted this behavior with whacks of a yardstick.

So Rosie learned to minimize the thievery at home where she was the prime suspect for anything gone missing. That fall, with everyone distracted by losing Mason, she branched out into the world. She got caught lifting some girl's ruffly umbrella from the school bus. That roused a stir. But a week or so later, she turned right-round and took a cherry-red lipstick from a teacher's own purse. It was mean Mrs. McCool, the choir teacher. Girl should of had her brain examined for that one. First my sister got suspended. Then she got belted at home.

When we were little, of course we all knew that our dad had a belt and it could be put to a certain use. But until the school called home to report Rosie's offense, we didn't have a clear notion what that use would be like in actual, personal experience. Jo Beth claims to remember Mason getting belted a time or two when he was around eleven or twelve. Then one fine day, later in high school, he up and slugged our father in the jaw (so she says), which put an end to further acts of corporal punishment.

I cannot confirm or deny.

Momma's yardstick on the bare backs of our legs could sting pretty bad, but we mostly knew it was symbolic discipline. At least, with me it was symbolic. I cried from hurt feelings more than from pain, so Momma didn't have to beat me real hard. I guess she may have gone a bit heavier on the other two. Rosie and Jo Beth would sneer and claim it didn't hurt a bit. Remorse was a rarity from them, in general.

But here came Mrs. McCool and her lipstick, a smoking gun discovered in Rosie's pocket right there in homeroom. When it emerged that she had stolen from a teacher, Momma stepped aside.

My sisters got home from school that afternoon, all unsuspecting. Jo Beth was instantly sent to the bedroom alone, the door shut behind her. And there stepping out from the kitchen was our father, home from work an unheard-of two hours early.

Our family has always lived in Devola. It was a sweet little town when I was a child. Still is pretty nice, I guess. But our father worked at Guarantee Tire in downtown Marietta. He would get home at 5:30 every night of the world, excepting

that day when Mason died, and now, when Rosie got suspended. She looked sick when she saw him come into the living
room. I'm sure she had the intuition of why he was home early.
Dad took her elbow and steered her through the kitchen to
the basement steps. Momma kept me next to her, on the divan. She put her arms around me. After the first minute, I hid
my face in her shoulder. She was saying the Lord's Prayer, her
blouse full of a smell that mixed lilac powder and hot Crisco.

We could hear everything through the furnace grate. Rosie
started sobbing right off, wet and juicy, even before the first
blow. Then the sobs turned to screams. It was a dozen hard
whaps! with a long pause halfway, while she begged for no
more and swore no fresh trouble.

All Dad said was, "I don't *never* want another call from
that school. You hear me? That school had better *never* call
here again!"

He said it after every couple of whaps.

Afterwards, Jo Beth and me tried to be sweet to Big Sister.
We smuggled in things for her to eat (since she got no sup-
per), but she wouldn't even look at food. Lying on her side
in bed, face to the wall, she made it clear she couldn't stand
the sight of us. We knew she was ashamed for us to hear her
cry. Eventually, she did drink a Sprite I brought her from the
fridge. Then she said, "Get lost, you little suck-up." But I was
glad to have some reply from her, at minimum.

Far as I recall, that was the only serious belting for any of
us girls. Rosie took it for the lot of us, but the message was
clear to all three.

Seems like it was the very next evening, our big sister announced at the dinner table, she would be going by the name
"Eff" from now on. "Effie" would be acceptable within the
family. She proved quite determined and refused to reply if
"Rosie" was uttered by anyone. Day by day, Effie she became.

Of course, this was hard on Momma. It all happened close to Christmastime, not a happy season anyway, so soon after our brother's passing. As I remember, there were a few gifts tagged for "Rosephanie" under the tree. Effie refused to open them, and there they lay, ignored, until the tree came down at the end of January. Momma unwrapped the packages herself and set the gifts in the bedroom for her hard-hearted daughter to find.

I think what Effie really wanted—being of a certain age at that point in time—was more of a tough name for going into high school. To be ready to hold her own. When the new name was still fresh, I once heard her tell the neighbor boy, "Yeah, I know what it stands for. And my middle name is YOU, so EF YOU!"

Warming up for the big league.

After Effie's encounter with the belt in the basement, our house went real quiet for a few weeks. One strange thing that happened during that time was our dog disappearing from his kennel. Our dog's name was Bowser-Boy, and he was a bird-hunting dog—some type of pointer, to the best of my spotty understanding. I do love dogs, and since my apartment won't allow them, I volunteer to walk the rescues at the animal shelter out on Van Camp Road. But I don't really know one breed from another.

Bowser was Mason's dog. I remember when we first got him, Mason would take me outside to toss a ball for him to chase in the yard. I was still pretty tiny and couldn't really throw, but Mason helped and encouraged me. I remember, nothing ever looked more joyful than that puppy leaping after a neon-green tennis ball. He would hurl himself into the air like life depended on it.

Once Bowser's hunting training got underway, we weren't supposed to play with him anymore. Dad said it would distract him from the serious discipline of learning to flush birds. That's also when the dog went to live in the kennel—as a pup he got to sleep on a pile of rag towels in a box in the corner of Mason's room. There were some fights over sending the dog into exile and a lot of whining at first from Bowser, but I guess he got used to it.

Us girls would sneak him little treats from time to time through the chain link. Stuff like strips of bologna or saltines. That was also a no-no, because it's real easy to spoil a bird dog's fitness.

Anyways, after Mason died, Bowser disappeared real suddenly—like somebody came and took him while we were out at the funeral, although I don't believe that's really possible. Daddy wouldn't talk about it. Momma only said, "He's gone to a better place," like the dog had died along with his master. I think Dad sold him to some hunter up county. Hope so, anyways.

But the biggest change that came along was when our dad got religion. That would have been around Eastertime the following spring. He decided major reforms were needed to break the whole family of slack morals and bad doings. Our conversion brought a stop to some of the fun things we used to look forward to, like get-togethers at Gramma Dot's.

Back then, I had no idea some of our relations might be considered "outlaws." Frankly, I couldn't tell Fannette-side folks from Twist. That history didn't get explained to me till later, maybe not till high school. But Daddy apparently thought consorting with such folks could be a bad influence. And for the big girls, that may of been true. Running with teenagers, Effie and Jo Beth might well of heard kids brag about stuff they shouldn't be getting up to, no way.

At first, while Gramma Dot was still living, we could still go to her house, but now there were rules—caution tapes to keep clear of. Like, we had to arrive and leave early, before things got to full swing. And we mostly stayed up at the house to visit with the old folks gathered in the parlor. Effie, Jo Beth, and me were forbidden to go off with other kids. That left us a lean bone, so to speak, but Dad's belt had created sufficient impression so any complaints were mumbled under hearing range.

And our church-going practice came into the plan. Not counting a few Jehovah's Witnesses and a branch of Nazarenes, the Howells have always been traditional Methodists. Momma took us to the First Church on Elm Street, and Dad would join for the holidays. But now, all of a sudden, he picked a new church that we had to attend three-four times a week. You could not get out of it unless you were down with genuine sickness.

I don't know how he chose The King's Way Holiness Church. It's one of the old independent Bible churches of Marietta—not a big megachurch like you see springing up along the Interstate. This was a small group of dedicated believers. Fanatics, I might call them now, but of course I didn't realize that back then. The preacher was a wiry little man with slick black hair named Reverend Bellamy. Ran the place like a patriarch of old, without help from committees or board members that I was ever aware of. He just told people what to do: You order flowers, you plan a special collection, find more Sunday school teachers, bring meatloaf next potluck. Whatever he called for got done at the bidding.

In the pulpit, his voice was like one long warning, and once he stepped down, he stayed dead somber. Only smiled at suppers and wedding receptions (never during the ceremony). In recent years, I've learned he started a television show, *One Hour Free From Sin,* in which he recounts the atonements unnamed members of his flock imposed on themselves to gain forgiveness from transgressions. Apparently, there were embezzlements, adulteries, gluttony, and death wishes. One drunkard cut off half his own pinkie finger to remind himself not to touch a bottle. And a woman refused to leave her house for years on end, lest she cross paths with the man she had lusted for in weaker moments.

I hear Reverend Bellamy has now earned himself a nice nest egg on the donations, embellishing those stories the likes of us used to tell. You see, the congregation had a practice we girls came to dread—a ceremony called "Contrition." It came in the middle of service about once a month, or as often as the Reverend deemed necessary. After a dire prayer calling on the Lamb of God to save our souls with His blood, people would come forward to confess their need for salvation. Many would kneel and weep and make all kinds of groveling prayers, casting themself as the worst sinner on earth and begging forgiveness. Some did this voluntarily. But also, anyone could be called up by others, like if some old man or biddy in the flock had spotted your car outside a tavern. You'd be expected to fess up and swear on The Good Book never to commit that sin again.

Yes, King's Way Holiness was a strict no-drinking church. It was also supposed to be no-smoking, but I don't remember anybody getting denounced for a cigarette. I bet they mostly all smoked at home, like my momma. She kept right on puffing out the back door. But then, Momma was already a strong believer and didn't need as much improvement as the rest of us.

Sometimes I've wondered if people honestly took those strict rules to heart. Were they hiding behind a Godly ideal nobody really lives up to? Thinking back, it seems to me our church drew in a large share of heavy alcoholics, folks who needed all possible help to clean up their act. That's a good thing—I accept that—and maybe it worked for them. Maybe that even included my father. Jo Beth and Effie both say so. Me, I don't remember him ever being drunk around home.

True, at picnics in the country, he used to sip whisky on the porch with the other men, Fannette and Twist alike. When the sun would drop to a deep gold slant and the youngest kids collapsed onto the nearest lap—those were the best times of all. But once his religious revival took over our life, there was an end to it. And he actually did give up cigarettes, far as I could tell, which everyone knows is the hardest thing to quit.

So now it was prayer before every meal. On Sundays, nine o'clock Sunday school and ten o'clock service. Fellowship dinners every week. Bible study Wednesday nights. Youth Group Thursday after school. And there were youth camping trips every other weekend in fair weather. The big girls hated those—too hot, too cold, too dirty. On the surface, Effie and Jo Beth made the best of our new ways, but they peeved and moaned plenty between themselves. I saw how they worked to get in with other kids, talking the talk like they'd done nothing but praise Jesus all their days. At the same time, they'd cop a racy attitude and toss off remarks that parents weren't meant to hear. Stuff like, "Slater is my favorite Christian!" or "R-rated movies teach you what sins to steer clear of," with that suggestive little smile.

Me, I didn't mind camping. I love campfire songs. Of course, when I joined the youth choir, they teased me no end. I remember Jo Beth saying, "Watch out, Britney. Here comes our little pop star." That type of thing.

It's not like Dad ever spoke about the reasons for our new religious dedication. He never said, "It's high time we quit those Twist folks 'cause they live in the clutches of sin." Didn't accuse anybody of selling drugs or running a poker room. Didn't announce that we wouldn't be seeing certain relations anymore. We just pulled away and left people to draw their conclusions.

In most cases, that was no big deal. Nobody was about to question how my dad decided to run his family. But like I mentioned, Dad's good buddy was Robert Franklin Howell, better known as Big Bobby. They grew up together and palled around back in the day—country boys that vowed to never work in town, nor kowtow to The Man. Of course, Dad became a grease monkey at the tire shop, and Big Bobby went the way he did, so they had already grown apart, somewhat.

I should explain that Uncle Bobby does *not* qualify as one of the "big-mean" Twist Howells by any stretch. He actually worked a fine government job at one time. County road crew. Then he got busted moonlighting with public equipment, not for the first time. It was a whole business—grading private drives, taking down trees at the horse farms with the bucket truck, and so on. A bunch of guys were in on it, but only one scored a stretch at Belmont. That was Big Bobby, 'cause he was crew boss. It was his first and only serious jail time. When he got out, he fell back on the time-honored combo of poaching, disability payments, and all-round self-reliance.

My momma still talked to Auntie Sue, keeping tabs on the family. Mostly they talked by telephone, but I know for a fact they would stop and pow-wow in the bread aisle whenever they both wound up at the IGA at the same time. There was a lot to keep up on, because we had five cousins over there (second or third, well removed, like I mentioned). I for sure never asked why we couldn't hang out with that bunch anymore, and to my knowledge the women never questioned things, either. It was just a new normal.

Sometimes I imagine Dad and Big Bobby passing on the street in those days, a quick nod and cool looks on their faces.

Maybe they would of stopped to spare a few words. Dad might claim we were all "same as ever," just too busy to turn up at Gramma's these days. I expect he would take on the sin of a lie to keep from insulting his cousin.

And, if that ever happened, how did Big Bobby take such a bogus claim? It's anybody's guess. Stuff gets left to fade away or fester, whichever it's gonna be, while years flow by.

As for the younger Bobby Frank, he raised his profile in my life when he came to check on me one time at the middle school. I was thirteen years old, and he was already polishing his local legend.

It was a memorable day.

Now, I was never real happy in school. I never went to kindergarten, even though my brother and sisters did. Maybe it's because, with Mason so much older and the big girls so independent, Momma wanted to keep me close. She just didn't send me. Back then she did different kinds of piecework at home like stuffing envelopes or prepping door-drop bags with ads and coupons. I helped her with that, and we would bake special desserts or get dinner ready, just keeping busy round the house. The big girls and I attended the same school for a couple years while they finished elementary. I liked having them there, casting that shadow of protection over me from the far end of the hallway. Nobody was going to pick on me with my sisters nearby.

Jo Beth was the one kids feared. She was known for tormenting little ones, boys and girls alike. Walking up the way, she'd pick a kid that had some funny look. One with fat cheeks or no friends—maybe new to the neighborhood. She didn't have to do much. Just spare a few choice remarks of belittlement and toss a lunch bag, here or there. She earned a big reputation that way.

One time, I saw her push a boy to the ground who wore braces on his legs. I told her she was too mean to live.

Jo Beth gave me a look like I'd never spoken before. Like she was observing some strange new weather phenomenon that she didn't much care for. She said, "I take it out on them so I don't have to beat *you*, LD."

I remember the pearl snaps flashing on the back pockets of her jeans, fluffy hair a-tossing, as she turned away. All that day at school, she never glanced toward me. No wink across the lunchroom, no gesture. Left me to walk home by myself. That put a damper on my desire to stand up for the less fortunate. But there were never any calls from school about Jo Beth's meanness, so evidently it wasn't as heinous as thievery.

You're probably thinking, penny theft and picking on first-graders is a far cry from what's broadly considered "bad behavior." Come on—when your average citizen thinks of a "bad girl," per say, it means just one thing, right? She let herself be touched before marriage, before engagement, or maybe not even in the confines of going steady! And she likely did it with more than one boy! For the popular mind, that's the worst a female can do in this world.

So it is ironic (if that's the word I'm after) that my sisters managed to become the kind of tough kids that insulated them from trash talk. From accusations of being "bad." What I mean is, they messed around freely where the sex-bases were concerned. But kids at school knew better than to spread gossip about them.

Me, on the other hand, I skirted every form of trouble like a plague. So trouble came looking for me.

Eighth grade, springtime. My sisters were up at the high school by then. I was on my own, and I'd been getting a dose of teasing from some girls in health class. They were looking for a rise of some kind, which I did not want to give them. Then one morning, when Mr. Davis mentioned condoms and how they could prevent "unwanted consequences," this girl who sat across from me started saying shit like, "Look at Howell—she knows all about it."

Took me a minute to believe she was talking about me. Her little minions picked up the chorus right away. They all stared, and some even spoke directly to me, which didn't usually happen. Their ill-attentions sent a shudder down my arms.

It was—

Show us how it's done, Howell.

You know how to roll it on! Get 'im good and hard first—

Over the eye and down the shaft, right?

Oh yeah. She knows. But she don't like to use it.

Mmmmm!

This went on, just quiet enough so Mr. Davis couldn't stamp it out altogether. After class, they blocked me in the hallway and cranked up the jabber so boys and bystanders, everybody all around, couldn't miss the show. And all over again: *Howell knows how it's done. Pinch the tip, right? She'll roll it on for you. She don't like to use it, though. Gotta feel that raw dog!*

I suppose they picked me for this treatment because I was embarrassed from the git-go, right when Mr. Davis held up the little square packet. Mean girls can smell that kind of thing. I don't know why it should of embarrassed me. I had never seen a condom "in action" in real life, let alone needed one. That's just how I was.

"Too tender," Momma would say.

Well, I knew better than to let the mortification show. I made my voice hard and told that ringleader-girl to get out of my face. Jeannie MacDonald, it was—daughter of a chiropractor, as if that makes you high and mighty around town. I told her off, but I didn't use profanity in those days, so maybe it wasn't convincing. They didn't go so far as to trap me against the wall, so after a minute, I pushed through the crowd and beat it to my next classroom.

Next morning, they had the welcome wagon ready. I came into school at the end of south hallway, which is closest to our street. By the time I got nearly to main hall, Mean Jean and half a dozen others were trailing me. There were guys, too, but at first it seemed like they were just in it to watch the proceedings, hanging round the edge.

The girls were talking that same shit. *Howell knows her condoms. Oh yeah...ribbed is best, right, LD? Too bad she likes to go without! You know what that leads to...*

And all the same as before.

Their voices started ringing loud, then soft, in my ears. You know, like reverb? The sound pounded with my heartbeat. They were getting to me.

The girls circled around me.

Then condoms came out of nowhere. Some were still in the foil, some unwrapped. Unrolled. Long and slimy-looking. Condoms came flying at me from all sides.

It's bad when you duck your head or put up a hand, like a spurt of blood in the water. One boy stepped in close—it was the noted class clown, Raver Conway. He grinned in my face, and people were nudging me closer from behind. Little shoves. My eyes went kinda blurry, but I saw him unzip and make like to pull the goods out of his puffed-up boxers.

Right then, from off at one side, comes flying a loose, waggling rubber that some bitch had filled with milky-looking goop. In hindsight, I can't believe it had, you know, real human fluid in there. Even at the time, it didn't dawn on me she could throw a bag of *you-know-what* right at my face.

Kids laughed and yelled in my ears:

Time to swallow, Howell—
You know what to do—
Drink it down, now—

I turned sideways by instinct. Just in time. The loaded condom glanced off my shoulder and fell with a *splat!* Oozy crap spilled out on the floor. Looked like Vaseline and chalk dust. A curtain of silence dropped long enough to crack the spell.

Looking back, I know I could of turned the tide right there. Somebody else could of come out the loser. I've pictured it a million times: I grab some side-girl, hanging back, get her arms behind her, and serve up the same kind of taunts they showered on me. I scoop that mess off the floor and rub it in her face till she spits.

Fun times.

Instead, I seized that moment to turn back where I came from, down south hall and out the door. I didn't run, didn't whine or cry, just swept like wind over low ground, straight on home. No one followed me, thank God. I didn't feel like a coward or a quitter, even though that's what I was, objectively speaking. I only felt like the world had gone wrong around me, turned into a dire, bad place, and I had to get away. More than anything, I wanted to be alone and hold perfectly still— frozen little rabbit in hawk's shadow.

Momma was out at the store when I got home. When she did come in, I told her I threw up in gym class. Spent most of that day lying on my closet bed. But my mind was blowing seeds in the wind, and one small thing stuck with me. Later on, after the fact, it stood out: Among those boys hanging around for the show, I'd noticed one kid that was plainly on-looking. Not joining in. You could see from his face, he didn't care for this business. That was my little cousin Dan, a seventh grader. We'd never been close and rarely crossed paths, anymore.

He was Bobby Frank's baby brother. I believe that recollection of the look on Dan's face was the only thing that gave me courage to get up and go to school the next day. Not that I had a plan, nor any real idea what to expect.

Walking out of the house that morning, I was praying Mean Jean and all of them would give it up and lay off. Of course, I knew that's not the way of the world. They'd seen I was on the run, so it could only get worse. Still, I put one foot in front of the other.

As the school building came in sight, when I crossed from our road onto Oak Knoll Street, I noticed a man hanging around near the entry door. It was a hunky young guy with lank, dark hair down to his shoulders, dressed in jeans and a plain white T-shirt. He was obviously waiting on something, leaned back against the buff-brick wall in the early sun. It occurred to me, this was a man of precisely the wrong age to be at a middle school—too old for even a held-back student and too young to have a kid in seventh grade. For a second, I started to veer toward a different door. Then, this man caught me with his eye, and I saw who it was.

At least four years had passed since we'd met up anywhere. He had filled out, grown the hair, but I recognized Bobby Frank.

Funny thing is, I used to think of him as way better behaved than his older brothers and, in fact, better than most of the kids we ran with out at Gramma's in the day. Bobby talked more respectful than a lot of boys, and he knew how to keep quiet for half a minute—like the old-timers might actually tell an interesting story now and then. That type of nice manners.

More recently, he'd got a different reputation, a Twist-Howell type of reputation. As I came closer, it seemed like he was actually cleaning his fingernails with a knife—some classic pose like that, but maybe it was my imagination. I don't really think he carried knives back then. This was before he lost his gun rights by getting on parole.

Bobby Frank gave me a kind of one-sided grin and said something like, "Hey, Sweetheart. Long time no meet'n'greet. You glad to see me, or what?"

I had stopped about ten feet off. After a second, I cracked a smile. "Sure, I'm glad."

He shoved off the wall and came down toward me. "Lemme feel it," he said.

I hugged his neck, planted a peck on his stubbly cheek.

"Real glad," I said again. In fact, I was over the moon.

Was the sweet Bobby I remembered a thing of the past? That question flashed through my mind when I recognized him. Even though our families didn't meet up anymore, I knew the milestones of his recent past: quit high school, got fired from the Foodway for making a load of steaks disappear, already served a couple disorderly charges, brawling at the tavern in Lower Salem and wherenot. At some point he'd taken up with the scary Torres family, a notorious bunch of outlaws based in Parkersburg. He even made a baby with Marlena Torres, who was at least a decade older than him and had plenty of babies already from her husband, Raul.

Raul was doing hard time for a car-scrubbing ring. I had heard Momma remark on the phone, *Let's hope the conjugal visits let Marlena pass it off as one of his.*

When I hugged his neck, Bobby gave a sigh. "Aww, yeah— Now, that's real sugar!"

He said all this time lately, he'd been missing the whole Elis Howell clan. So today he just stopped by to walk me to homeroom for no special reason.

"Would that be a good idea?" he asked.

I said it would be an outstanding idea. Bobby swung the door wide and held it open like a gentleman. We strolled inside. Right off, I spotted my welcome committee loitering around an open locker up the way.

Scanning the hall, Bobby kept us to a leisurely pace. He asked me friendly stuff like, "How's my Uncle Elis keeping these days? We sure missed you'uns at Easter, LaDene. Tried to save you some lamb cake, but you know how that goes."

Mean Jean MacDonald and her bitch crew visibly froze stiff as we came close. A couple of girls who'd been on lookout turned toward the lockers real quick. I saw that Raver Conway and another boy were there among them.

Bobby saw the boys, too. He moved lightning fast. "Hey there, Li'l Pal! School days going good for ya?"

Bobby reached right through the bevy of girls and seized Raver by the shirtfront. He lifted the kid up on tiptoes.

Now, Bobby is not a small man, as I'm sure you noticed. He was pretty lean back then and totally ripped. Imposing, you might say. Holding a punk like Raver off balance with one fist was something he could do all day long. He dragged the boy in this position to the middle of the hallway.

Bobby kept talking. "'Cause I would hate to hear that things were going badly for you here at school. Ya catch my drift? Git what I'm saying, Li'l Pal?"

Raver sounded like the half-crushed squirrel in Old Owl's claws. "Yeah. Sure. I know. Yessir." He croaked out words to that effect.

"Okay, then."

Bobby shoved Raver down, butt to the floor, and left him to scuttle aside like a crab. He turned to Raver's friend, Jimmy Decker, who was standing by, back plastered to the wall.

"You, too, Shrimpy." Bobby faked a half-lunge in Jimmy's direction, which raised a gasp from the kid's throat as he bolted up the hall. Disappeared into a gaggle of kids outside the cafeteria.

Chuckling at this handiwork, Bobby actually reached down to help Raver back to his feet. The boy muttered things like, "I'm fine. Thanks. All good." He managed to walk away, fast as dignity allowed.

At that point, Mean Jean took it in her head to make a stab. "Hubba-hubba," she said in a hoarse half-whisper. You could tell it was a certain kind of play—going for a sexy voice but with her nerves twanging. Her half-shut gray eyes fastened on Bobby's chest, ventured up toward his face.

Bobby Frank touched the middle of my back, real gentle. He said, "It's up to you, LaDene."

Mean Jean could see what was coming, but she just had to stand there and take it. No doubt, she thought I would slap her face, but I'm not so good with an open hand. I put my weight behind a punch to her stomach that deflated her like a blown tire.

Thanks, Effie, for teaching me that the hard way.

Cousin Bobby walked beside me all the way to homeroom and said good-bye with a stroke to my hair. "Don't be a stranger, hear?" he said.

And out the building he slipped, before the office got wind of an intruder in our midst.

* * *

OKAY, I GUESS YOU'RE PRETTY BORED with the deep background. On to the "day in question." Was it just yesterday? Hard to believe.

It was a Friday, end of a long hot week. Marietta was muggy as a jungle, like usual. I worked a seven-to-four shift at Riverside. Like I say, I've been employed there since I turned eighteen. Long enough to get a full weekend off, which I was looking forward to. So after work, I stopped at the Foodway to stock up.

It was my usual day-off haul: rack of precooked ribs so I don't need to turn on the oven, salt and vinegar chips, box of sour cream donuts, a bottle of Smirnoff, and that pomegranate juice I like to mix it with. I got no use for orange juice.

So you see, I was expecting an ordinary Friday night at home, relaxing by myself. Not planning on going much of anywhere Saturday, either. Typical low-key weekend. In no way did I expect the events that took place instead. How could I have?

When I got home and pulled into the parking lot, there was a shade spot under the linden tree at my end of the building. That felt like a stroke of luck, even though I wasn't planning to drive out anywhere again before Sunday. That's when I visit Momma and Dad in Devola. They're still in the house where I grew up. Once or twice a month, I go see them.

Of course, I parked in the shade spot.

Grocery sacks in hand, it took me a minute to juggle my purse and keys at the entry door. I've been trying to remember if I sensed anything. Some premonition. Seems like I should have, 'cause ever since I've lived at Haven House—since I moved away from home—I've had thoughts now and then of what it must be like to come home and find someone lurking inside.

An evil-doer wishing harm, waiting to strike. That happens more than we like to believe, especially when women live alone. I'm a great consumer of true crime dramas, so naturally, that stuff occurs to me.

There's an old story my Gramma Dot used to tell of coming in to find a strange man, some scary wildman, hiding in her family's house. This is my Great-Grandmother on Dad's side that I'm speaking about, Dorothea Howell Becker. She's the one lived on Duck Creek Road, in the house I've mentioned, where the incident I'm coming to takes place.

When she was a girl about twelve years old, my gramma came up from the field one afternoon to fetch water for the family. They were all out hoeing beans. Nobody'd been back to the house since dinner, and naturally it was standing all unlocked, as was the custom. They thought nothing of it.

The way she told it, young Gramma pumped water in the bucket, much as she could tote, and dropped in the dipper for drinking. Then a thought popped into her head—a thought of leftover biscuits with a big drip of honey from the jar on the sideboard. She was sure there were at least three biscuits wrapped in a towel in the mixing bowl. So she banged in the side door, into the kitchen, and opened that towel with biscuits inside.

While the honey rolled off a long spoon onto the crispy top, she got to wondering why the housecat didn't stroll over with a friendly *mmrrr!* quivering her tail the way she usually would do when somebody came home after a few hours quiet. In fact, the house seemed extra still. Or maybe there came a slight shift of floorboards. Gramma looked to the parlor door, some eight feet away. There wasn't much vantage into the room, but she could see Kitty crouched under a caned chair, fur on end to twice her size—eyes like saucers fixed on a spot young Gramma couldn't see. A spot along the near wall, just behind that doorframe.

That cat was not usually scared of man nor beast.

When the cat saw Gran looking her way, she commenced to growl like a mean old dog. All a-tremble now, the girl leaned away from the sideboard till she made out a reflection in the front window. She saw a skinny, mean-looking fellow in raggedy garb with wild hair—some vagrant or crazy man. He was pressed against the wall waiting for whoever might come through the doorway. Gramma thought he had an ax clutched across his chest.

When she told it, she used to say, "My mind saw an ax, but I cain't be certain if that's what he had or not."

She dropped the honey spoon and flew across the kitchen in one jump, back outside and down the field to her family. I guess her daddy kept a shotgun with him or in the barn, because he was able to arm himself before heading to the house to sort things out.

All he found was a line of muddy bootprints. They didn't belong to the family, because the left foot showed a patch on the sole that didn't match anybody they knew.

The cat stayed spooked for days.

Now, that's just a quaint story from the era before door locks. Tame compared to the dramas of today. But here's the kicker: Gramma's family got an awful shock a day or two later. News spread that an old couple in a cabin out by Whipple Run turned up murdered in their bed—their son came by to help out around the place and found them. As the story goes, their faces looked peaceful, but they were hacked to death—the whole bed drenched in blood.

Hearing all that over the years has made me take stock of what really can happen right when you think you're in your own safest place.

But like I say, yesterday afternoon when I came down the inside corridor and got my apartment door open, nothing of the sort crossed my mind. I walked in and, yes—I caught a whiff of something not quite ordinary. Something like stale cigarette smoke, the way it gets in your clothes. But I can smell the fresh smoke when my neighbors light up on their patio, so I didn't think much of it. The place was stuffy—I don't run AC when I'm out for the day, and odors can build up in the heat.

Nothing new ever happens to me. Why would it start now?

I stepped past the coat closet into my living room, turned toward the kitchen, shopping bags hanging from my hands. I was thinking about those salt and vinegar chips, followed by a long cold drink.

But whoa—!

There I see a large man leaned back on my divan. Legs splayed in old faded jeans, splotchy green T-shirt stretched across his belly. Dark hair straggling over his ears and forehead. And there's his pack of Camels on my coffee table.

An elevator lurches in my stomach. I take a step back. One of the grocery bags hits the floor with a *thunk!* My vision goes blurry, like my eyes are trying to erase what's in front of me. I'm not the kind that enjoys surprises.

The man moves, raises his eyes. He might of been dozing. True, that's not the most sinister behavior. But now I'm putting a bad face on him—the face of a serial killer. All the bad shit I watch on TV these days.

I'm telling myself to turn and run, but my feet are like roots in dry ground.

The man gathers himself. Leans forward slow, pulls up his knees, and rests an elbow there. Raises a hand toward me.

"Hey, LaDene. Aren't you gonna say 'Hi'? I been waiting here to see you. Been waiting on you since noon, Miss Darlin'."

I know the voice. It helps me settle down to where I recognize his face. Bobby Frank Howell. He heaves up from the divan.

"I apologize about your sliding door. I'll take care of that. Fix it for you."

My eyes follow the wave of his hand to the patio door. I see a slash cut across the screen, a jagged chunk broke out of the glass, long cracks crazing away from the hole he must've reached through to flip the lock.

I take another step backwards. My face must register alarm.

Bobby Frank crosses the floor that fast. He jams me into the wall, forearm under my neck. He grips a wrist and holds it tight to my side. I go breathless, cold, even though I see his eyes are laughing.

This is just some funnin' around. Ha-ha. I manage to say, "The hell, Bobby Frank—" Like I told you, I do dog-walking for the animal shelter to keep half-way fit. But right now, I am struggling for breath.

Bobby laughs. His arm slides to the back of my neck and turns the roughhouse into a bear hug, smooshing my tits against his well-padded ribs. He's definitely put on some fat, but his arms are hard as tree trunks. And he smells surprisingly clean, a whiff of Ivory soap, under those smoky clothes.

I give him some pats on the back and push out of his grip. I try for a strong voice, say, "You coulda called me on the phone, couldn't you? 'Fore you busted up my door?"

He laughs, gives me a buddy punch on the shoulder. "I don't have your number, LaDene."

I am not used to manhandling, and it leaves me a little dizzy. Months at a time nobody so much as touches my hand. Yes, I turn my patients over in their beds and get them up into chairs, things like that. But nobody reaches for me most days. For pride if nothing else, I try to disguise my shakiness by tossing my long braid over one shoulder. Like you noted before, this makes for a good-sized gesture.

Bobby takes it in, says, "Last time I seen you, you's living at home with Mommy 'n' Dad. How'm I s'pose to have your new phone number?"

That can't be right. I'm sure me and Bobby met up about five years ago, when I stopped at his folks' place in Lower Salem. That would of been after Uncle Bobby had his stroke, paralyzed him down the left side. Momma thought I could give some professional advice thanks to my health-care credentials. We brought Aunt Sue a cake and an envelope with fifty dollars. Lots of folks were visiting at the time, but I remember for sure Bobby Frank was there. We sat out on the porch together, talked about nothing in particular.

I figure he's recollecting a different occasion. Then I look close and realize from his face—eyes going half-closed and popping back open—he may not be in any kind of right mind.

"What've you been doing in here all this time?" I ask.

"Nothing so awful, LaDene. I don't do the meth. Don't touch it. Nor the Vike and whatnot. Whatever folks may say about me."

He picks up my grocery bags off the floor. I reach for them, realizing I'd just as soon he not find that large bottle. But he's not to be denied. He carries the bags to the counter that divides my kitchen from the living room. Taking a peek, he says, "Well—Looky here!" The plastic handles splay apart, and the bottle stands tall. The chip bag blossoms like a pillow. "That's more like it, LaDene, Sweetheart. There's the welcome home a man deserves."

He bends close and aims a kiss at my mouth, which lands off to one side as I angle my face away.

It was coming clear to me that Bobby Frank had lately been released from the Belmont CI. I knew from Aunt Sue that he'd got five years in 2015, robbing one of the Quick-Marts off I-77. Word was, he only snagged a hundred dollars and a case of Sudafed, but the prosecutor threw in gun specs and gang activity (procuring meth fixings) to boost the sentence. If I'm right on all that, he must of served two mandatory minimums and got an early release.

Bobby is rummaging in the freezer compartment. He finds my ice bin, and fills two tall glasses from the cupboard.

"I know you weren't planning on company, Darlin'. I'm messing with your routine. But hey—" He takes the vodka by the neck and gives a hard twist. "I'ma fix you a real nice drink, and we'll take a breather. Shoot the shit. Okay?"

I microwave the ribs, divvy them between two plates. Pour half the bag of chips in a bowl and run water on a couple of dishrags for hand-wiping.

Bobby pours one glass two thirds full of vodka, which is flat crazy, adds a modest topper of red juice. Watching me with a wacky eye-roll, he tips up the bottle and draws from the neck, shakes his head like a mad dog, and sprays vodka toward the sink, but of course it goes every which-way.

"Hooo! Sorry—" He wipes his mouth on his forearm,

laughs, clowns around like he's going fall on his ass. "That Russian shit ain't my drink!"

He looks in the fridge. Pours his glass full of ice tea and takes both out to the coffee table. He sits down in his spot where he was before, stretches out one leg to reach in his jeans pocket. Pulls out a good-sized prescription bottle.

"This here's my relaxation." He gives the bottle a little shake. "Puts me right in The Zone."

I look at the rib plates pooling with barbecue sauce. Normally, I eat in the kitchen, on a stool at the counter, but Bobby's already getting comfy on the divan. It feels too late to make him come perch on a high stool. Oh, well. I carry the food out to the table, go back to fetch the bowl of chips.

Bobby leans close to where I sit catty-corner from him on the loveseat.

He says, "I'll share with you, LaDene." I can see that the pill bottle cradled in his hand holds an assortment. Looks like mostly Xanax. Also some Ritalin, one of which he fingers out of the collection and washes down with tea.

I shake my head. "I don't do no kind of pills, Bobby. You wouldn't either, if you knew what's best."

It's true that I do not do pills and have no intent to start. I only recognize the drugs, thanks to my nursing work. But you don't need to be a medical expert to figure this is not a great start for someone fresh out of jail.

"Well, get your drink on and let live, LaDene." Bobby whacks my upper arm with the back of his hand. He grins, lifts his chin toward the insane amount of vodka he poured for me. "I'm sure you know 'what's best'."

He makes a whimpery face, then mugs the look of an overeager five-year-old—till I can't help laughing a tiny bit. My eyes blink shut like I'm being really patient. I pick up the remote and switch on the tube for background while we eat.

The evening news drones about a three-car pile-up on the Interstate, then a Marietta councilman accepting favors from a business in his ward. There might be a "recall election," even though his fellow councilpersons say it was no big deal. Current temperature is still 83 degrees. A thunderstorm, rolling up from the Gulf, may bring heavy rain to our region.

Bobby sucks a rib bone. He says, "You didn't write me up at Belmont, LaDene. I kep' hoping you'd write. Momma said you did stop out to see her and Daddy while I was gone. That's sweet of you. I thank you for that."

I am sipping my drink. Sweat has started to pool in the middle of my chest, under my bra. The overhead fan is going, and the busted patio door is wide open, but there's no real ventilation to be had.

Bobby seems to read my condition. "You're still in uniform, girl. Don't you let your hair down when you come home?"

He makes like to reach for my braid.

"Watch your gooey hands!" I lean away, toss him one of the damp dishrags. There's a bone and many barbecue drips on the coffee table. I take my plate to the kitchen.

"Sor-ree," Bobby says. "It's just, I'd sure rather see you in civilian clothes, y'know? I been up to here in uniforms, if you get my meanin'—" He chops the side of one hand under his chin.

It's true, I'm still in blue scrubs from work. Why shouldn't I change? Normally, I would of done that by now.

"Back in a minute," I say.

There's two fans in my bathroom to keep the humidity under control, a ceiling vent and a small one I keep on the tank of the commode. I switch on both, then realize that I wouldn't be able to hear footsteps over the whir. I lock the door, hoping the TV in the living room will cover the sound. But why? What's my problem? This is my house, I can lock doors as I see fit.

I strip down, the air feels good on my skin. But something

stops me from turning on the shower. Water pouring down would fill up my ears, and I picture the door busting open, shower curtain flying away—Now, stop that. Bobby Frank wouldn't do a thing like that. I perfectly well know he wouldn't, but the notion cramps my style, regardless. I soak a washcloth with cool water, sprinkle it with cologne.

Guess I'm just not used to having anybody in my place, let alone having a man here while I clean up. My family never even comes here. My dad has not once stepped foot in the place. Momma visited a couple of times, when I first moved in. Brought me an old set of dishes and some flatware. But really, why would they need to visit me? Dad likes Momma's cooking best. He doesn't like to eat anywhere but his own home. They're set in those ways.

When I go see them up in Devola, usually one or both of my sisters shows up with some of my nieces and nephews. Sometimes their husbands come along, too, if it's a special occasion. I imagine what they'd say if they got wind of the scene I'm in right now.

I can hear either of them—Jo Beth or Effie, one—saying, "It's LD and Bobby Frank, sittin' in a tree! Well, well—"

Okay, so? I always liked Bobby Frank. That's no secret. Back when he saved me at school, he was a hero to me. I'm well aware he's got—what? Two or three kids by now, by different women, not one of which he ever supported or even lived together with. And those pills he's popping is gonna make it extra hard to get any kind of sensible act together. Poor Bobby. Is all that any reason to shun the man? Who's gonna help him with the trouble he's waded into?

I hang my head and mop myself off. It's just clean sweat, right? I showered this morning and stayed in the AC all day. Sip on my drink, having brought it in here with me. I'm enjoying the fans sending sweet breath over my skin. My nipples stand up. I rinse the cloth and wash between my legs, let the excess water splatter the floor.

Okay, I'll admit—I am thinking of Bobby, of him being just outside my door, and I feel something. So what? I am not the brain-dead white lily who would let some shit happen. I am not an idiot. Not that we are such close kin it would be wacked-out hillbilly shit for us to hook up. No, not that. It's plain crazy from the standpoint of who we are and what we could ever be to each other. No one needs to go looking for train wrecks.

I slide the elastic off the end of my braid, comb damp fingers through the strands, separating the sections, till I have a long, wavy cape down my back—I push it off my face with a rolled bandana from the top drawer. My favorite lime green. Twisting it into rope, I pull the hair over one shoulder to leave my neck cool. Find clean undies in the laundry basket, jean shorts and T-shirt from the door hook. As you can see, these shorts are long, almost to my knees. Summerwear, but not what you'd call sexy by the standards of today. I swig my drink and head back out.

There is Bobby, down on his knees, taping the side of a macaroni box over the hole he put in my sliding door. Masking tape and scissors from my utility drawer lie on the floor alongside unused portions of the box. I wonder where he dumped out the macaroni. C-plus for effort!

I say, "That don't even fit good, Bobby Frank. It'll run up my electric bill if I put on the AC."

Bobby rocks to his feet, leaves the supplies where they lie. He swipes his pills off the coffee table and pockets them. Says, "Okay, girl! Let's blow this hot box and go for a drive."

As you know, I drive a Fiesta, which is not the world's greatest ride, though it does have basic amenities like AC. But when we get out to the car (in that deep linden shade, remember?), there's a breeze picking up from south of the river.

Leaves are rustling. So I start up the car and roll down the windows. With a nice tire squeal backing out, I inspire Bobby to yell, "Woo-hoo!" as we hit the street.

For a minute there, it felt like I was a young kid, the kind of girl I barely had a chance to be, out for a fun night with fun people, just taking a look at the world. We could go anywhere, try anything, 'cause this was our town, and we belonged. I keep my radio tuned to the station that rotates between country and oldies. It felt like a good sign when the Grateful Dead came on mid-chorus. *Sugar Magnolia.* Bobby set to drumming his knees.

I didn't drive far, just over the Putnam Bridge, cruised the historic district—the Castle, the Basilica, past the fancy old mansions from the oil boom era. Deep flowery gardens, and streetlamps of old. Enormous shade trees, magnolias and buckeyes. I rarely come over this way anymore, but I used to love it here. Makes me feel like there's something worthwhile in the world, you know? Like once upon a time, people built a few things to last, whether I'm looped into that life or not.

True, Bobby soon dampened my mood by asking what kind of stash I had in the car.

"I don't keep no illegal shit in my car, Bobby Frank. Can't we just be in the moment without that?"

"Yeah, yeah. I know, right?" He rummages in the door pockets, glove box, under the seat, till fate lays his hand on a paper sack full of mini-bottles, about a dozen, various kinds. I had honestly forgot they were there. I've got a coworker who heads to Florida for two weeks most winters. She shares those with me from the airplane. Just being neighborly.

"Al-*right*ee—that's what I'm talkin' about!" Bobby spins the top off a mini Crown Royal, and it's bottoms up.

Yes, I will say this injected a note of concern into my sense of good clean fun. I'm confident of being competent to drive, myself, since I didn't half-finish all that vodka he poured, but Bobby is obviously a volatile compound. I'm sure the last thing he needs is gas poured on a Ritalin fire.

I tell him, "You know liquor's a bad combo with the pills you got there, right, Bobby?"

"I ain't washing nothing down, am I?" He puts his hands up, gives me that mischievous kid look, like, Yeah—we both know I'm pushing, but what you gonna do about it?

I don't want to peeve and be a downer. So I keep my eyes on the road.

Bobby's palm comes over and strokes my thigh up and down. He says, "That's what I'm *really* talkin' about—you in those shorts, Sweet Girl."

"Let's keep this show G-rated, okay, Bobby?"

"Okay. Yes, ma'am. I mean, Mom."

But my leg is tingling from the touch, even through stone-washed denim. I'll admit, one part of my brain had been wondering, if Bobby just got out of jail, why he didn't jump my bones right off, back at the apartment? Or maybe he got out a week ago, and he's already been to see the Torres woman or some other baby mama he used to hang with? That could of took the edge off.

I ask, "We could drive out and say 'Hi' to your folks. Is that where you been staying since Belmont?"

He blows air. "Daddy's a wreck. Momma's wore out with it. Too depressing."

Hmm. There's a non-answer for you.

I turn down the Sacra Via, back toward the river junction where the Muskingum joins the Ohio. I pull over on Front Street and kill the engine across from the Riverside Commons—the greenest place in the world and the coolest outdoor spot in our muggy summers.

"C'mon," I say. We pile out of the car.

There's families out and about on benches, pushing strollers, kids chasing around in the declining sun. Light sparkles on the river current and scatters dollops of gold on the grass under the trees. Just think—the folks across the street have all this in front of them every day of the year. Right here, there's a sweet old brick house with a deep balcony on top of the porch. White shutters. It's not grand like the oil barons' mansions, just old-timey and homey-looking. As a girl, I used to daydream of living in that very house someday.

Bobby intercepts a whirling Frisbee and spins it back to some teenagers up the brick street. We sit our butts down in a clearing between honeysuckle bushes.

"So this here's LaDene Howell's secret power spot?" he says. "Your special place where you rule the world?"

I scoff. "Not hardly."

"Your folks used to bring you kids down here?"

"Not much." I stare at the muddy waters, let the sun-glints hypnotize me. "But there was one time," I say. "We rode down here on bikes all the way from Devola. Right down Highway 60." I shake my head at the wonder of this—such an improbable memory. But here it comes, flowing into my head. A beautiful day, birds in the sky, happy people. "It was before Mason shipped out to basic. A Sunday morning, about this time of year."

Bobby gives a chuckle. "Can't feature your daddy on a bicycle."

"It was all Mason's idea. I think he rented the bikes. There were tandems for Momma and Dad, and one for the big girls. I rode with Mason on a bike with a child's seat. We wore these dorky neon-green vests for safety, but there wasn't much traffic to speak of at that hour."

"People still in church?"

"No doubt. We rode right down here to the Commons,

and we ate sandwiches—I think we sat at that table over there by the historical sign. Momma brought a Tupperware of macaroni salad. Thermos of coffee for Dad. And Mason played tag with us girls. I remember running my hardest, and I knocked Effie right down on her hands and knees. Totally by accident. Mason wouldn't let her pound me. It was a crazy fun time. Afterwards, we rode on downtown and got ice cream cones. We walked right under the Ohio River bridge."

Just then, I'm thinking it may have been the last time I saw my parents smile at each other. The only time I can remember, at any rate. There at the picnic table, my dad put his arm around Momma's shoulders, and they gazed in each other's eyes like young lovers. So sweet.

"Mason was a good 'un. The kind that die young."

I give Bobby a sharp look, but he has dropped his head, playing with a grass blade, and I think he's being serious. Not smart-alecky.

He goes on, "I looked up to him a whole lot back then. Don't know if you would of been aware. Out on Duck Creek Road, he was always my favorite of the kids a little older than me. We used to squirrel hunt, sneak beers, trap fox—try, anyways. All the country-boy games. I never thought nothin' we did was bad or wrong so long as Mason was doing it, too."

Bobby fishes a cigarette from the almost empty pack in his T-shirt pocket, lights it with a match from a little cardboard box. He offers the last cigarette to me, but I decline. He shakes two fingers at me with the lit smoke.

"I had every intention to follow Mason into the Marines. When he joined up, I was still in school. Wanted to kill terrorists and serve my country, just like him. Hard to believe all that now. What if, what if—I think about it a lot. Your dad sure changed when he lost his boy. Wasn't long after, my daddy got nabbed in the bucket-truck caper. If none of that shit had of happened, we'd be different people today."

"Who?" I ask. "You and me would be different? Like how?"

Bobby squints hard at the sparkling water, like a magic fish might rise from the ripples and offer us free wishes.

"Our dads used to be buds, right? Grew up together. When they pulled apart, it hurt my family more than you think, LaDene. You remember all that business with the 'Misuse of government property,' right? What people don't realize—my daddy took the fall to spare a bunch of guys that were involved to the eyeballs. One of which was the upstanding manager of the Guarantee Tire Shop. Who do you think passed him those jobs on the horse farm and shit? Who replaced a wrecked tire off the books to keep that good thing going? Sorry to break it to you, Sweetheart. Your old man was on that operation from the git-go."

This was news, but I couldn't say it surprised me. Maybe kickbacks were part of the sins my dad needed to work off with the big reform movement. It made sense there might of been more than one reason for our religious revival.

"Hate to disappoint you, Bobby, if that's why you're telling me. It doesn't really pack the wallop of shockwave-type news."

He smiles, leans back on his elbows and drags on the cigarette. "I know, Darlin'. I'm just putting it out there. Backdrop of what mighta been. I mighta turned out a better man if I didn't go for the quick cash with my daddy in lock-up. Mighta done it all different."

"You are a good man," I say. What did I mean by that, exactly? No idea. Just seeing where things would go, I guess.

Another smile. His finger traces a circle on my knee.

"I could use a sweet young girl. One that wouldn't mind some visits from her stepkids. Couple of her own? The simple life." He laughs. "Could *have* used a sweet girl, that is. Bit late at this point."

I should of said something hard, like, "I ain't sweet by nature. Not what you'd call all that young, neither." Instead I manage a laugh and try some questions.

"So you got no plan to fly right, now that you're free? Find real work, save up, and all?"

"Nothing's impossible. So I'm told." Bobby flicks his smoke toward the river. Lumbers to his feet and reaches down a hand. As I get up, I thought he was making a grab at my ass, but quick as a fox, he lifted the keys from my back pocket.

He puts an arm around me, steers us toward the car. "Let me drive. Okay, Sweetheart? Since I'm such a good man."

No, I don't believe Bobby had any specific plan at that moment. Certainly not one that involved Principal Rutherford. His mood was still mostly light-hearted. He was joking around when we got back in the car. Headed up Third Street in a northerly direction.

Yes, that is the direction toward the Speedway, and also Devola, Coal Run, and numerous other places where we did not wind up going.

Once we are rolling, I make another play for information. "So are you a true Twist-line man, allergic to old-fashioned job-type work? You know the magnet plant nearly always needs people."

Instead of obliging with a real answer, he breaks into song. "Don't worry, don't worry, Mama…" He pats a rhythm on his knee and croons.

I get into the spirit with a laugh.

"But you're the one with a voice, LaDene," he says, out of nowhere. "I know you got some pipes. Won't you sing one for me? Some nice old song?" He punches the radio off to clear the air waves.

This takes me by surprise. When did Bobby ever-even hear me sing? I give him a scowl. He gives back that puppy-dog look. Riffling through my mind, I hum a bunch of random notes, clear my throat. Eventually, I sing a few choruses of "The Green Leaves of Summer." Half of the first verse. It's one of my favorite songs from when I used to perform in a girls' group, back in my teenage years. One of the nicer things I've ever been known for.

After I stop, Bobby gives me a ton of props, like how I should be on the stage and need to cut a record. And ought to be headlining some church choir—all that BS. He reaches over and touches me again, kind of a half-hug around the shoulders.

I am smiling like a ninny. By this time, we are cruising up Muskingum Drive.

Bobby says, "What say, let's pay a visit." He hangs a right on Rathbone Avenue.

Why here? I get a sick feeling.

We are rolling past those sweet little 1960s houses—three-bedroom ranch-style with trim front yards. Low porches. Mailboxes down by the street, draped with flowering vines. Bobby slows way down. Is he bringing me here on purpose? I do happen to know someone who lives on this block.

He pulls over in front of a house with brown and beige siding, big picture window, mini spiral-type trees on either side of the front door. It's got white rail fencing in the corners of the yard, with roses growing over top.

I always liked that storybook look. Snow White and Rose Red. And I know this particular house. I used to drive by sometimes. Not for many years, now.

Bobby shuts off the motor.

My eyes are glued on the dashboard. Bobby's looking at me, and I know he can see me breathing kind of heavy. How does he know what this place is to me? His arm slides along my shoulder, hand drops onto my hair, gathers up a lock.

He says, "Our mommas talk, you know, Darlin'. They prob'ly shouldn't, but they talk between theirselves."

Such a thing is not news to me, but the thought that mommas' talk might leak beyond the two of them makes me purse my mouth.

Bobby points with his head. "This is his house, ain't it? His house with his wife?"

I don't move, nor answer. No one has the right to make me look back on ancient history, over and buried. But then, I'm the one who let Bobby take my keys, and watched him drive right up to this door, ain't I?

You see, the man who lives in that house with his family— wife and three kids, last count—was briefly a friend of mine in high school. In fact, if you don't count Bobby Frank being my hero in eighth grade, this high school friend was my first love.

And the only love of my life so far.

* * *

BERNARD O'BRIEN WAS THE ELDEST son of a family that owned— still owns, so far as I know—a whole slew of businesses around Washington County. They lived out in Devola, where I grew up. What you may not know about Devola is that it's a very mixed town. There's what you'd call "an enclave" of rich people in fancy new houses with river views, there's still some old farms along the oxbow, more or less prosperous, and then there's the rest of us, ordinary folks in the middle of town. The O'Briens did better than most with their Ford dealership and auto parts store, as well as the Guarantee Tire Shop and Service, where my father happened to work for our living.

My dad's immediate boss was a brother of old Mr. O'Brien. So it wasn't quite like I was dating the boss's son when I started seeing Bernard, which Dad and Momma would surely have frowned upon, had they known at the time. But it was pretty damn close.

Bernard was called Burner around the high school, although, in fact, he was a clean-cut and sweet boy, not a
burnout type at all. Good student, track star. The first time I
saw him—really saw him—he was practicing sprints on the
school track, leaving the other boys so far behind they might
as well just go on home. It was a fine spring day. He was a
fair-haired boy, and the sunlight on his blond head made me
think of an angel flying down to earth. All that summer, as I
looked forward to starting high school, I dreamed about going out with him, going to a prom dressed up with a flower
on my wrist, all the trimmings.

It was nice to have a dream.

Of course, he wouldn't notice the likes of me. For one,
he was two years ahead of me. Not to mention he's from a
rich family, the kind of boy that's going to college. We were
not in that class. But in spite of everything, the two of us did
come together.

We never dated, per say. He never took me to a dance or
movie or nothing. We didn't have friends in common that we
might of run with as a group. After all, I was not the outgo-
ing kind and had never really dated at the middle school. But
against the odds, we crossed paths that fall of my sophomore
year. It started at a sock hop after a football game the week
after my fifteenth birthday.

The dance was winding down. I was hanging around till
the group of girls I palled with decided we were ready to split.
Kids in couples, or the ones who had hopes of getting next
to someone, were waiting for the last romantic slow song. It
started at last—"Baby Hold On" by the Dixie Chicks, one of
my favorites back then. Bernard happened to be standing with
his friends in my field of vision, and when I heard that song,
nothing could of been more natural than to raise my eyes on
him—the angel-haired boy I'd dreamed about since last spring.

That's when a miracle happened because, somehow-some-way, Bernard glanced at me, right in the same moment. Our eyes hooked, and he didn't hesitate more than a second—he walked right over to me. The gap between us was, maybe, twelve feet, but it felt like he was flying across the whole Ohio River to a separate world where I was living my little-small life.

He put out a hand. His face had a sweet, kind of lopsided, grin. His voice said, "Shall we dance?"

I had never heard anybody, let alone a kid around my age, say a thing like "Shall we dance?"

Now, I know—and more or less knew at the time—he might of been looking to make some other girl jealous. I saw one or two of them, back where he'd been standing, drop their jaws when he put the move on li'l LaDene Howell. But why would I care? It did not cross my mind that this was anything less that a gift from God.

When I took his hand, I stepped into my Cinderella story. His touch shot a bolt through me that felt stronger than the hardest drink I've had in my life—if he hadn't taken me into his arms, I doubt I could've kept upright. My knees were that weak. But he kept the hand I put in his, pulled it to his heart, so my breasts fit on either side of our wrists. My temple came to rest on the front of his shoulder. His other hand and all his fingers traced the bones across my back and settled on my shoulder blade. I thought I might grow wings and really be like him. I know he must of felt me tingling all over. His slightest touch had done that to me.

When the song stopped, at first I couldn't raise my eyes. After a moment, I followed his hand lifting mine to his face, and he planted a kiss between the knuckles of my first two fingers.

He said, "Aren't you from Devola? One of the Howell girls?" In that euphoric state, it didn't cross my mind that Effie and Jo Beth's reputations might of preceded me.

I nodded, or maybe I said yes, although it felt like I couldn't possibly use my voice right then.

He kept holding my hand and kept talking. "You like to hang out at Devola Lock and Dam? Me and my friends go there a lot. Come out this Sunday, if you can."

He gave my hand a final squeeze, turned away, headed back to his friends. The world could of ended right then and left me happy. But he glanced over his shoulder and said out loud, "Thanks for the dance!"

To me he looked like the happiest, most carefree boy that had ever lived. I wanted to eat that like a last meal.

It took a little while for us to wind up together.

That first Sunday I rode my bike to the park to meet him, it was like he said—a bunch of kids hanging out in a group. Boys from the various sports teams that were known as arrogant jerks. A couple of girls on the benches—the fashion-plate type that belong to clubs, daughters of lawyers and judges. Some brandished cigarettes and blew puffs in a showy manner. I stopped while there were still shrubs along the roadside to hide me, listened to the boys' loud laughs, the girls giggles, and didn't go up to them at all. I turned right-round and rode home.

But all that week, I reviewed how Bernard had looked at the park in khaki shorts, his powerful legs in sockless boat shoes, wide forearms emerging from an oversize blue T-shirt. So clean, so relaxed—shooting the breeze with wide shrugs and grins. Not smoking. Clearly a nicer boy than the company he kept.

So the next Sunday, back I went, down the narrow asphalt road. River water pouring over the dam filled my ears. Sitting on top and around the lone picnic table, it was more or less the same group from the week before.

It was a gorgeous day of early fall, no longer hot but still sunny, still warm, trees barely touched with yellow and rust. I told myself I had as much right to hang out at the lock as any-body. Sure, I did. My family used to stroll over here, evenings. My dad took his boat out on the river all the time. My sister Effie claims he took us fishing almost every weekend when she was little. Too bad none of that made it into my memories.

But while I hung back debating myself, Bernard caught sight of me from where he was standing by the picnic table. I still remember how his arm shot up above his head, and he waved real wide like he was signaling somebody off in West Virginia. And he called to me. He had found out my first name. He called me by my name: "Hey, LaDene Howell—!" And he smiled real big.

I was pretty near a total fool at that point, but it made a nice impression that he wasn't ashamed for his friends to meet me and see that he had some kind of fondness for me. I knew it meant he was a nice person deep down. Honest to God, I still think so, no matter all the shit that was soon to meet the fan.

It turned out, the boys in Bernard's crew were actually quite interested to hear about my family. The notorious Twist-line men, that is. Everyone has heard tales about some of my relatives: Jake Blaine Howell who used to pimp out his own wife and sisters, back in the day. Old Eustis Howell who did a murder for hire in 1987. It never occurred to me that those connections could spark people's interest in my own self.

I was happy to confirm that, yes—my uncle was Big Bobby Howell who'd come home from Belmont just a cou-ple years prior. And, of course, renowned bar-fighter Bobby Frank was my cousin. I omitted the fact that my own family had cut ties with most of them years ago.

It only struck me as a little scandalous that those boys on the picnic table were swigging from cans of beer. Bernard soon pulled a bottle of pink wine out of a backpack. He twisted the cap off and handed the bottle to a girl sitting across from him. There were no glasses, so she drank from the neck and passed the bottle to her friend. That one drank and passed to me. I tasted it—my first alcohol. A couple of turns had me knocked pretty near on my ass.

Everything about hanging with this group was so new to me, I really didn't notice right off when the party starting breaking up. Or rather, it started breaking down into couples who scattered here and there, down to the cove to make out under the willows and on the little sand beach by the river.

The odd boys out shuffled off to a black and chrome Silverado pickup parked on the asphalt. The driver revved his engine and drove away down the road. That's when my wish came true—Bernard was alone at the table with me. We talked a little more, I've no idea what about. In years to come, I would review every touch and sensation at least ten-thousand times, but I can't recall a single specific word we exchanged. I just knew that he was being sweet, not mocking me, or treating me like a lowlife hick, regardless who my family was. I talked a lot more country than him and his friends, but he showed no sign of caring a snap about such things as pronunciation or community standing.

Of course, sex was not a secret to me. Momma had explained many times which body parts were involved and that it was the number-one thing girls must deny boys as a sacred duty. Jo Beth and Effie teased me in the privacy of our bedroom, telling all the details of their exploits. One time, I remember Effie asking me, "How many times you been fingered, LD?" The answer was zero, but I was so horrified she might think it had happened even once, I pressed a pillow over my head. Naturally, she only said it for the fun of freaking me out.

So I had learned a lot of racy things, but the upshot was I viewed sex as something dire and disgusting. When I fell in love with Bernard, it truly didn't cross my mind that what I was craving with him was sex. I utterly believed this was something higher, some fine and beautiful destiny. I could no more have turned him down than I could of stopped the sun in the sky. All told, I went out to meet him by the river six weeks in a row. I looked back later and counted up every meeting on the calendar. He took time to kiss me and hold me. He pressed me up against the wall of the pump station, and he brought along a soft plaid blanket for me to lie on.

I thought I had discovered a lovely new world that held a special place for me where I would live in grace from then on, lonely no more. Indeed, a new life did open for me. Just not the one I imagined in those mad romantic days.

* * *

BUT RIGHT NOW, BOBBY FRANK is leaning close with his hand gentle in my loose wavy hair behind the bandana. I can feel his eyes looking into my soul. I hear him give a deep sigh.

He says, "Don't ol' Burner O'Brien need reminding he's got a past like everybody else? He's got a kid he never met out roaming the wide world somewhere? One he swept under the rug?"

I give a scoff of disgust. You know nothing about it! I want to tell this nosy cousin. Instead, I raise my eyes to stare out the windshield and say nothing.

"Ya see, LaDene, bad shit that's happened don't float away on thin air just because we want it to. You'd probably feel a whole lot better if you sounded off a little. Don't you think?"

I look at him now. "Let me understand you, Bobby Frank. You're saying I should go knock on Bernard O'Brien's door after all these years. After twelve years when I haven't spoke to him or hardly laid eyes on him. I should knock and yell and embarrass him in front of his family—?"

"I'm sayin' it might do you good."

"Do me good? It would embarrass *me* more than him!"

"Shouldn't he face the music? Shouldn't his kids by Marion Whatsername find out they've got a big sister by LaDene Howell?"

My breath is burning in my lungs. I glare at Bobby and grit my teeth.

"It is a girl, right, LaDene? A sister to his kids."

I raise my voice. "He's got no rights. None whatever. He gave up all rights." I surprise myself with these words. I don't normally think of the sad past in terms like these. It's entirely irrelevant what "rights" Bernard may or may not have.

But Bobby seems glad to take my point. "That's it, LaDene—damn straight. Shouldn't you let him have it, for your own sake? Tell him off—one and done!" He brushes his hands against each other: Good riddance.

Again I sniff and look out the window. I can hear Bobby take and riffle in the sack of mini-bottles.

"Here," he says. "Liquid courage." He pops the top off a Smirnoff vodka and hands it to me. The drink does steady my nerves, which had gone into a jangle.

"Hell," Bobby says. "I'll go up there and tell him off, if you won't. I can't stand the thought of him skating through life like nothing ever happened. These people who think they're top of the crop."

"You are not going to that door, Bobby Frank."

"I am. I will, LaDene."

Before I quite decide, I am slamming my door behind me. I hear Bobby emerge on the driver's side.

"No way in hell!" I glare at him over my shoulder. "You stay put."

He leans against the car, raises his hands—have it your way. "I'm here if you need me," he says.

* * *

MY PURSE IS OVER MY ARM, and I reach in for a breath mint so I won't smell like a drunk at Bernard's front door. Of course, I have no intention of yelling at him or reminding him in any way of long-buried drama. Thank God, the front yard is deep—I've got several steps to go while I come up with some excuse for being at his house, and hopefully, Bobby won't be able to hear what I come out with. There are lights on in at least two rooms of the house.

I'm out with my cousin who's back in town lately, and your name came up. We're in the neighborhood. Thought I'd say a quick 'Hello'--

I can picture Bernard cracking a little smile, maybe offering me a glass of cold water. Or would he ask his wife to serve ice tea? I don't doubt he'd try to act cordial, even though, inside, he'd surely be mighty confused and nervous. Does his wife even know about me? Our history?

I have no intention of shaming people. But now that I'm almost there, it is tempting to just take a peek. No turning back.

I ring the bell by the door, a heavy golden oak job with square windowpanes. The chime is a little church-bell melody. I wait long enough that I figure Bobby can't fault me giving up. Nobody home. Aww, too bad! I resist the temptation to look around at him standing back by the car. He's liable to come up here and pound the door a lot louder.

Then I hear steps and the door swings open.

I could tell it would not be a man, the steps are too light. It is the wife, a short-haired blonde woman, very slim and fit. In fact, she's wearing tight shorts and a striped tank top, like she might of been in the middle of a workout video. I'm not sure of her name. I never met her. She didn't go to our high school. At least, not while I was there.

"Can I help you?" she asks. Not cold, but not especially friendly, either. She stares like I've got two heads.

I say, "I'm an old friend of Bernard's." Nearly short of breath, I forge ahead, praying desperately in my heart. "Is he home by any chance?"

"No, he's not at home. What is this about?"

Praise Jesus!

I see her look past me and her face registers the presence of Bobby Frank out by the car. I picture him giving a nice wave, but I don't turn to check. Let's just wrap this up.

"I am the class secretary of Marietta Unified High School. Class of '06." I'm not good at doing numbers on the fly, but that should be the year Bernard graduated. My heart pounds, although at this point there's not much on the line. "I'm collecting for a gift for the school on behalf of our class—a nice concrete bench to put out front by the flagpole. A bench with a plaque." This level of detail actually impresses me, just running off my tongue. Don't know my own creativity, I guess.

"So I just wondered if he'd like to contribute. But since he's not here—"

"He's away for the weekend," she says, "but I can give you something." Ever so slightly put-upon.

"Oh, no. It don't matter."

"Yes. I'll save you a trip, stopping back by." She reaches out of my sight to what I suppose is a hall table where she keeps her purse. Comes back with a ten-dollar bill in hand.

"Oh. You don't have to," I say.

"You're collecting, aren't you?" She holds out the money.

I take it. Say, "Thank you."

"What did you say your name was?" she asks.

"Jo Beth Howell."

"I'll tell Bernie you stopped by, Jo Beth Howell."

The sun is dropping, setting off an evening glow by the time I turn around. There is a piece of folding money in my hand—what a joke! I feel a smile coming on as the O'Briens' nice oak door shuts behind me.

Bobby Frank is grinning my way.

"You took money off the bitch? La*Dene*—you are all that and more, Baby Girl!"

"Knock it off. It was ridiculous."

But I can't help laughing along while Bobby holds the passenger door for me. Getting in on his side, he slaps his knees, keeps saying I'm the bomb. He's well entertained. I can see that he downed another Crown Royal or two while I was putting on my show for Mrs. O'Brien. I celebrate with a Cuervo Gold.

Bobby starts the car and cruises slowly toward Colgate Drive. I can feel a "but" brewing.

He says, "Gotta face your fears, li'l cousin. Right? And I am proud of you. But that wasn't the confrontation per say that we had in mind, now, was it? O'Brien not home, sad story goes untold. C'mon—you got off light!"

Dear God, what now?

"Ya see, LaDene, I'll admit it—I get some bad thoughts in my head from time to time so I know how that shit can weigh a person down. Like I say, back when you were little, our families were close. Our dads were more like brothers than whatever kind of cousins they actually are. Then, *shaz-zam*—we never see you'uns no more, like you moved away to California or something."

He fishes that last, lone cigarette from his pocket and flips it between his lips, then slides it behind his ear, instead.

"And, ain't it almost more your daddy's doing than O'Brien's that you got sent away and lost your baby, or whatever it was that happened? I don't pretend know the whole novella, start to finish. But what say, we drive out to Devola and have us a palaver with your old man? How's come he never went to see his old best cousin who's half-paralyzed from strokes now, huh? How come his baby girl was never the same after that long trip he sent you off on? I'd like him to explain some of that shit to me. Talk things out like realistic people. Let's do it. Let's pay a visit."

"Honest to God, Bobby, I would sooner drive straight into that tree than take you out to my folks' house. Think about it—we been drinking, you're on pills, and it's not going to happen. Forget it."

"Okay. True. We're a bit lit. We needed the relaxation. But this is serious. If we're ever going to shape up and live right, we got to face the demons. Exorcize the demons."

"Speak for yourself, Bud. I work a steady job. Pay taxes. I'm as shaped up as I'm gonna get."

"C'mon, Sweetheart. Just a friendly 'Hello.'"

I decide it won't do to try and yell sense into Bobby Frank. He wheedles around me, regardless what I say. So I grab the near side of the steering wheel and pull toward the curb. Bobby cooperates for once, stops the car.

I lower my voice, try and make him understand.

"Bobby, my dad don't hardly speak to me, as is. I go out there on Sundays, sit, eat, chat with Momma, watch some TV, help weed the garden or some such. If he says five words to me the whole time, it's a good day. But now, you're saying I should bring you in, all hopped up, and ask why he got religion, why he shunned Uncle Bobby, or did this and didn't do that? He's liable to not even look at me anymore. He might decide I shouldn't even stop in next time. Is that what you want for me?"

"How did it happen, LaDene? How exactly?"

"Oh, y'mean my dear Aunt Sue didn't spill on that?"

Bobby ducks his head, says, "I just thought, maybe, you'd like to unburden. If you want to."

If I want to. "Okay, fine." I decide I'll spill some more guts if it keeps us away from Devola. "Let's go somewhere for a serious chat. Drive on back to the old cemetery. The Indian mound." Recollection tells me, Bobby's first arrest was there. Age seventeen, with some guys from his old crew.

"Sure," he says. "That's my favorite spot."

The western sky is still bright with sun shafts rising over the southwest hills. This is lucky for us, since the sign says, *Daylight Hours Only.*

We walk under the iron arch of the fancy old gateway, its bronze letters declaring MOUND CEMETERY. Bobby assures me him and his high school buds were just smoking pot, hanging around till midnight for the sake of bragging rights, not doing any vandalism on the Revolutionary generals' monuments. Never!

Past the old stones with angels and urns carved on top, down the narrow lane, we come to the steep steps that lead to the top of old Conus, as every Marietta kid knows the earth mound is named. Up we climb and down we sit, beneath the pines, on the marker where our local fathers buried a time capsule almost fifty years ago.

Another 50-some to go till whatever they thought mattered back then is revealed anew.

Bobby rustles a couple bottles from the sack he has brought from my car. Hands me what turns out to be a Gray Goose. With a quick, crisp swipe, he raises a match to light his last smoke.

Squinting into the flame, he says out one side of his mouth, "Go girl. Tell all."

* * *

AT AGE 15, I WAS A PURE-D ninny who imagined I was flying with angels rather than having sex per say. There was zero chance I would slam on the brakes, think real careful, back up and obtain appropriate precautions. The fact that Bernard likewise didn't intercede in that process has always told me he was a little bit swept away, too. Yes, that's probably my emotional comfort food, but I believe it, regardless.

What happened was predictable enough. Within weeks of our first encounter at the Lock & Dam Park, I was pregnant by Bernard O'Brien.

As deeper autumn weather set in, meet-ups at the park dropped off. Me and Bernard never did walk together in the halls of school, or sit together in the cafeteria, but he still made eyes at me across hallways, dropped the occasional sweet note in my locker, and stopped to chat on the stairs before class. He always said he was thinking about me, missing me, maybe we'd go out somewhere next weekend, and sweet nothings along that line.

All such moments, fleeting though they were, let me keep faith that our special times would, somehow, start up again soon. I won't belabor the weeks of bewilderment, then the agony of fretting, after it dawned on me that I'd been having plain old sex, after all, and it had produced its natural consequence. By the time I admitted this stark fact to myself, I was almost four months gone.

Me and my momma had always been close. Of course, I was nervous, but not altogether wrecked, at the prospect of coming clean with her. I knew she was the one to help me figure out the next appropriate step. From my perspective of today, it's embarrassing to confess that, in my heart of hearts, I thought me and Bernard would simply get married—happy ever after. I didn't know how it should all get arranged, but the outcome seemed inevitable in my mind. Such a stone-cold delusion.

I waited for my moment when only me and Momma were home, a weekday afternoon. She was having a cigarette in the kitchen. I went and stood in the doorway, and all's I said was, "Momma?"

Real quick, she turned to look at me. I guess my voice alone had said it all. Her eyes got this focused look, and she scanned me, up to down. Then her shoulders kind of sagged. She said, "Sweet Jesus. Don't tell me."

I could see she had figured it out.

She asked who had done it. I swore Bernard O'Brien was the only one. I think a shadow crossed her face when she heard the name, but she didn't remark on it. Then she asked, How did he treat me? I understood that she wanted to know, had I consented to the deed? Did he treat me like a girlfriend that he cared about? I admitted to consenting and swore he'd been most kind. Then she wanted to know, How many times? Which I lied about, shrinking the number of our meetings considerably. But I thought I had to say it was more than once or else she might not believe I had really consented.

I didn't want to get Bernard in trouble. Overall, I think Momma got a pretty clear picture of how things came down.

"I love him with all my heart," I swore. "And I know he loves me, too."

Only then did she cross the kitchen from the backdoor and give me a hard slap across the face.

Her voice was harsh. "You've been a pure-stupid girl. And a sinner." She told me to stay put in my room and not make a sound till I was called. "Take yourself some crackers," she said. "I won't be calling you till after dinner."

For the moment, I felt a great relief. The worst was off my chest, and Momma hadn't yelled at me to speak of. I believed she would protect me, far as she could, from my father's wrath and sisters' scorn. She would know how to manage things between the two families, and best of all, me and Bernard would soon be setting our wedding date. Images of a lacy dress and lily-flowers uplifted my spirit. I actually fantasized about a cute little apartment where we'd set up house. Didn't the O'Briens own a building on Ferguson Street, behind the hospital? A vacancy would open up by magic for their son and his bride. Yellow eyelet curtains and a red braided rug.

I sat gazing out the bedroom window at the bare gum tree in our backyard. Soon enough, I heard Daddy come home from work, slam the door and stamp wet leaves off his feet. Then I got a little jumpy and started pacing the floor.

My big sister Effie had taken a place in town by that time and wasn't living at home anymore. Jo Beth was out waitressing most evenings, or running with her friends. So I was glad, at least, the sisters wouldn't witness my downfall as the family good girl.

Let me skip the details of Daddy's denunciation, which made me cry hard as a hailstorm, and Momma's caution that I breathed a word of my predicament to a soul at my peril. Confinement to the bedroom continued for another two-three days. I stayed fairly upbeat, flipping through magazines, occupied with my tin-foil dreams of wedded bliss as Mrs. O'Brien. Momma let me come out for meals while Dad was at work, and Jo Beth held her tongue when I didn't get up for school in the mornings.

Looking back on those in-between days, it's like I was the girl sleeping under a glass coffin lid, oblivious to all things of this world. On about the third morning, Momma called me out to the living room and told me how things would really be.

She cried a little. I was too shocked to cry until later.

The O'Brien boy would not be marrying me. Not now, not ever. Compared to the rest, that part did not floor me as bad as one might expect.

I would be traveling out-of-state to a church-run home for girls who'd made grievous mistakes like mine. I would go there alone—leaving my home and family behind for the first separation of my young life. At that distant place, I would stay for the next many months—as long as it took for me to be delivered of the misbegotten baby. Mr. O'Brien had kindly agreed to foot the bill for my travel, residence, and medical costs. On the condition that no details of any such arrangement would ever be disclosed to a single living person.

Once this plan was formed, I never really saw Bernard again. He didn't have to come to our house and fess up to taking my cherry, or apologize for failing to use protection, or explain why he wouldn't be making things right. Two weeks later, after what passed at our house for the Christmas holiday, I departed for Missouri. In the meantime, I wasn't permitted to attend school nor hardly leave the house (lest I whisper to somebody the secret of who had knocked me up, I suppose). Over this time, my father wouldn't look at me. After his angry words that first night, he didn't speak or acknowledge the corrective measures intended for me. Momma gave me dinner those nights before he got home from work.

The day before my big trip was scheduled, as exile came to feel like a very scary reality, Momma let me know that Jo Beth had agreed to take some days off work and ride the bus with me to Missouri. As an official adult at age nineteen, Jo Beth would make sure everything was shipshape at "the facility." She would see to it that I got settled, and report back home to Momma and Dad.

"She'll be nice about it," Momma promised. "It'll be a good chance for you girls to talk."

Part II

When we got dropped off at the Greyhound station, Jo Beth had recently colored her hair the dark red shade that was popular around that time. She wore a short, shaggy cut that made her look oh-so-trendy in tight jeans (in spite of her weight, which had spiked since she finished school), high-heel boots, and a bright red parka. In my oversized jeans and gray Marietta College sweatshirt, I definitely felt like a pathetic stepchild. I don't think I looked pregnant yet, but the center of my body already felt like a box you can barely get your arms around. My legs felt tied together at the ankles, and head like it was packed with cotton. My heart felt like it'd been beat with a stick.

We boarded the bus and staked out seats in the front third. Jo Beth carried her large hobo-style purse and a tote bag. I guessed she was bringing a change of clothes for herself, but I didn't ask. All I had was a backpack stuffed with sets of underwear, including an unopened 12-pack of maternity undies, and a simple flannel nightgown. Momma had gotten word that I shouldn't bring any other clothing of my own, nor any books, phone, radio/music-player, keepsakes, or etc.

As we embarked on the highway, Jo Beth provided a lot of distraction with her usual running commentary. She likes to sound off about every aggravation that occurs to her, even before serious inconvenience gets a chance to build. She had comments on the people around us—their ratty clothes, stinky bodies, shifty eyes, and stringy hair. Then there was the insane drivers on the road, either crawling like turtles or racing like maniacs. More interesting to me were the various sights whipping past, from massive Hummers on display at lavish dealerships to empty hick towns. Jo Beth pronounced these even more boring than Devola, if such were possible.

I glued my nose to the window whenever she spared my attention. All the world slipping by—trees, towns, fields, pastures—gave me a numbing comfort. Not quite everything had collapsed, after all.

Daylight faded as we hit Indiana, but I could see it was a state of far fewer trees than I was used to. The sunset was red and purple, long flat clouds reflected above the horizon. Then it was night. Jo Beth napped for an hour or two. A lonesome farm light shining across the fences, near the silhouette of a small-town water tower, made me think, for no reason, of a porchlight somebody might of left on just for me. To light my way.

It would be somebody who loved me best in all the world. Once upon a time, that was my momma. Now I knew I had nobody like that anywhere. It made me cry for a long while, off and on again, quiet as I could.

Jo Beth woke up looking around like there'd been some loud noise, but in fact, the bus was peaceful. She broke out a Coke from her tote bag, still cool enough to enjoy, I guess. I munched a peanut butter sandwich she offered me. After a minute she decided we should move back to an under-populated area where we could have vacant seats behind and in front of us. An elderly black lady snoozed audibly across the aisle. That's where my sister figured we had sufficient privacy for her to announce the following—

"You're gonna hear some things eventually, so Momma wanted me to go ahead and fill you in. Soon as I get back from taking you to the girls' home, me and Jay McLaughlin will be tying the knot. I'm sorry you can't be at the wedding, but you won't be missing any grand occasion. We're just going to the Parkersburg courthouse, so nobody much will notice the date. Yes—" Her voice dropped to a near-whisper. "I *am* pregnant, but not so far along as you. That's why Momma took your news hard—figures she failed to teach either one of us a blame thing. Which is true, the way she sees it! Well, at least I'm with a guy that can marry me. Look, I'm on your side, LD. It's wrong for the O'Briens not to step up and do right, but you gotta face it—that Bernie you hooked up with is just a kid. And not the kind to quit school. Oh, I know, he's cute and no doubt a sweet guy. I get how you could go for that. But it wasn't a match, so what can ya do?"

As she delivered these indisputable facts, my sister actually placed her hand on my arm, a show of affection she rarely bestowed, and her voice took on a confiding tone that I had only ever heard from her one time before. When she first met Jay was the only time I had heard it—last year when she was still in school. She begged me to cover for her sneaking out our bedroom window to go meet up with him. She got the sweet voice then, seeming to need me to believe she'd found the treasure of true love with this 30-something-year-old weekend musician from Huntington. After all the nights she ran off to be with him, I would've thought they'd have to get married quite some time ago.

The part that came as no surprise was that Jo Beth wanted to keep things on as strict a down-low as humanly possible. She still attended church at King's Way Holiness with our dad and momma, so she had to hide her sins under a bushel, on pain of public shaming. Effie had long since quit King's Way, after she got called to account in the middle of Contrition for her car being noticed with a bumper sticker that said "WTF," in reference to George Bush ("W," that is). Not only blasphemous language (implied), it disrespected our God-appointed President, so Effie had some 'splainin' to do.

I understood full well this was the same reason why I was headed two states away with my thick ankles and bread-dough belly. Yes, I accepted it. Bowing out quietly should be easier than living under the judgment of everyone I knew, and everyone my family deemed important. But would it actually turn out any easier? That kind of thing is tough to measure, isn't it?

Meanwhile, Jo Beth was still talking.

"—good thing I'm ready to settle down. I can switch to part-time at work, take a few months off. The restaurant is good about that. And Jay loves me, gots a decent job—"

He worked maintenance at a paintball range, which I suppose is decent enough.

"It's a good time for us set up house, get me out from under Daddy's thumb. That's one heavy thumb, girl—ya know what I'm sayin'?"

She landed my arm a whack with the back of her hand, trying to get me to join in a grin at her much awaited escape from our father's strict oversight. But she wasn't done yet dropping mind-bombs of unexpected news. Turning on a dime, her face went somber, and her whisper grew hoarser still.

"You must never tell a soul, so help you God, LaDene—I'm gonna let you in on a dark truth. This is actually my second time." She glanced at the empty seat behind us. "I got pregnant right away when me and Jay first met. Back in school, like you. My senior year. He took me up to Columbus, to the Choice Clinic. There was no other way. I mean, I hadn't even graduated yet." She gave me an intense look like I'd imagine you get from somebody who's threatening your life. "Momma and Daddy have no idea. Besides Jay, Effie's the only one who knows. She gets it. And now you. So this is our secret. Just us girls."

I felt myself getting short of breath. A little queasy.

"But I told Jay—no way: I will not do that again. It's

wrong, and I really don't believe in it. So now's the time to make it official. Start our family. I laid down the law."

Jo Beth must've noticed my head drooping and the hard draw of breath I took right then, 'cause she sprang into action, got me on my feet and helped me to the lavatory. She was good at playing the pulled-together Big Sis who knows how to handle things when little girls get the nausea from sins they never should of done.

* * *

SINCE IT WAS ON PAIN OF DEATH that I knew, I didn't reveal to Bobby the part about Jo Beth's secret first pregnancy, the one I'd been told to keep a deep secret. But I told him the rest of those episodes, so he just might gain a mote of insight and lay off the whacked-out notion of dropping in on my parents for a little recreational confrontation.

While I shared the account, Bobby kept shaking his head. About a dozen times, he said, "That ain't right, Sweetheart. Shouldn't of been that way."

To my surprise, it did feel good to "unburden." It actually made me feel high, almost happy in a weird way. Maybe "transported" is the word I'm looking for. Here I was talking about things I'd never spoken of before, not once since they happened a dozen years ago, but nothing crashed out of the sky. No unearthly power rose up to fill my mouth with dirt, stuffing the words back down my throat.

* * *

THE BUS RIDE TOOK FOREVER. Meal stops were short. People were snarly. Twicet I thought Jo Beth was going to pick a fight with some lowlife black men in the far rear seats. Since this was occurring in January, there were cold drafts on the bus and frigid blasts every time we stepped off.

I took note when we saw the sign welcoming us to the state of Missouri, since that's where I was destined, but JoBeth said not to get excited because we still had to ride clear across it. The city of St. Louis caught my fancy. We rounded the bend of a hill and I saw city lights reflecting off the big silver arch. I overheard a pair of ladies say that the arch represents a "Gateway to the American West." Of course, we had learned since grade school that Marietta, Ohio, was the gateway to the West. Now it came clear to me that there's a whole further region out that way, which I hadn't doubted, but never before sensed as a real, existing place. There were old brick buildings alongside of super-tall skyscrapers over the waters of the Mississippi River. Some local kids had written multi-colored words I couldn't decipher on the railroad bridges. For about half a minute, I felt a sort of excitement. Like my life could turn out in a good way, after all—maybe someday I would come here to live in the big city. I would get a nice job in a bank or something. More pipe dreams to keep my mood up.

Mostly under cover of dark, we wound our way across Missouri. I saw enough to learn that it's a pretty region of hills and rocks, a lot like back home. Everything was edged with light, lacey snow. There were loads of billboards for caves and caverns that were evidently the points of interest. I have always hated the idea of going down in some dark cave. Like being buried alive. As we passed these signs, I couldn't help picturing gaping holes in the earth, dropping away all around the highway—every time I closed my eyes it felt like I was falling into nothingness.

Getting comfortable proved impossible, but eventually I fell asleep, regardless. When we came out on the west end of hill country, the sun was rising behind us, shedding yellow light over the rolling snowfields. On the side roof of a half-ruined barn someone had managed to write in big letters, "A noble wife is worth more than rubies."

Jo Beth said we were getting close.

We changed buses in Kansas City, another vast metropolis, full of black people. I wasn't sure what to expect after the rude men on the bus, but at the station they paid no more mind to us than if we were invisible. From there, it was a short backtrack on a smaller-type bus to the town of Rich Hill. That name proved ironic, as the place appeared to be at least half-ghost. I never thought of Ohio as a wealthy state per say, but parts of Missouri made it look like Buckingham Palace.

We got off at our final stop on a narrow street between grain elevators and an abandoned-looking collision service. We were supposed to be met here by someone from the New Dawn Ministry, to whose care I was being entrusted. On a peeling bench by a broken sidewalk, we waited for what seemed like forever. At least the sun rose higher and snow was sparse, although the wind was sharp as a knife. I could see Jo Beth getting crosser by the minute, so close to the end of her duties, but she held her tongue for once.

After half an hour or so, we saw a pearly-colored Lincoln Town Car roll slowly around the corner. It pulled up to where we sat. The woman who emerged from behind the wheel wore a drapey white coat open down the front over one of those pantsuit-type outfits that would later be made famous by Mrs. Bill Clinton. This lady's suit was a pinkish-orange color that set off her platinum blonde hair, which was held in one of those immobile, curly styles favored by elderly women, although I'd guess she was only around fifty, herself.

She didn't ask who we were. Just announced in a deep, gracious voice, "I am Mother Margaret Fitzsimmons. Headmistress of the New Dawn Ministry for Christian Girls." She extended her hand to Jo Beth. They exchanged some pleasant words.

Mother Margaret Fitzsimmons looked at me without extending a hand. She said, "And this must be our new little ward. Welcome to New Dawn, dear. We're so happy to have you joining our family."

I badly wanted a bathroom before getting into another vehicle, but the tiny Greyhound office behind us had proved to be locked. Getting the backseat of the large car to myself was my consolation prize.

Jo Beth sat up front. She and the headmistress entered upon a contest of interrupting, in which the rules seemed to require that neither betray any show of exasperation at getting talked over by each other. Jo Beth emphasized that she would need to inspect the housing where I would be accommodated. Our parents were expecting an account from her when she returned to Ohio. And she needed a printout of "The Rules" for sending letters and gifts and talking to me by phone.

For her part, Mother Margaret Fitzsimmons ignored most of this and offered no promises. Instead, she talked at length about the "spiritual needs of girls this age." Praise be to God, The New Dawn Ministry had a detailed program for addressing these needs.

"Prayer. Service. Reflection. Discipline. These are the Four Pillars of our Program. They uphold the formation of godly young women," she explained.

Toward the end of our twenty-minute ride, she glanced over her shoulder at me with a startling smile of perfect white teeth. "I know you're going to love it at New Dawn. People say it's like a summer camp. Do you like puppies, dear? Our Golden Lab, Mindy, had a litter of ten last week. If you settle in real nice, I'll introduce you to Mindy myself. Let you see those dear little puppies."

The New Dawn Ministry Headquarters might, indeed, have looked like a summer camp—with the headmaster's three-story home, a church building, three long bunkhouses, and other farm-type buildings, all painted pure white—except that you don't expect camp to have ten feet of chain-link all around, topped by double-angled, triple-strand barbwire. This "campus," as we were supposed to call it, was set on a lonesome road, four miles from the last village, amid cattle pastures and stubblefields.

In the parlor of the big house, Mrs. Fitzsimmons relented and gave Jo Beth some printed literature on "The Program." Evidently, when Jo Beth and I had boarded the Greyhound back in Ohio, my family knew almost nothing about this place. The Headmistress then told us to wait until "a trustee" showed up to escort us to my bunkhouse and begin my orientation.

"God be with both of you girls," she intoned, and disappeared up the stairs.

I was feeling hungry, shaky, and too shy to ask for a bathroom, so I was stuck waiting out that discomfort a while longer. It wasn't hard to tell that Jo Beth was unhappy with many things, most likely including Mrs. Fitzsimmons's tone, and maybe also the look of that barbwire outside. We'd entered the compound through a rolling gate that the headmistress opened with a device on the visor of her car. At the same time, it was obvious from Jo Beth's murmurs of "How nice" and the like, that she felt a need to maintain the semblance of a positive outlook. As if all this would be just great once I got used to it.

From out front of the house came the sound of a pulley clanging in the wind against a flagpole. I wondered where the dog and puppies were holed up. Someplace warm, I hoped.

In a burst of air scented with the prospect of fresh snow, a gray-haired woman in her sixties, dressed like an old-time farm wife in denim jumper and plaid flannel jacket, came in through the heavy glass-and-wood door. A person of few words, she led me and my sister outside, across a patch of winter lawn and the gravel road we'd drove in on, to the first in a row of low structures that I'd already guessed were dormitories. Inside, the large room was only heated to about fifty degrees.

Mrs. Anders, as she introduced herself, pointed to a bottom bunk right in the front, "Where new girls start out." She implied that I might earn a bed farther away from outdoor drafts as I gained seniority. Several items were folded and stacked on the bunk waiting for me—sheets, pillowcase, a blanket, towels, and several items of clothing.

"You should change now," she told me. "So's I can take your old clothes to the laundry. You'll get 'em back when you graduate."

She sent me to a large, freezing washroom with a group shower like in a school gym, two extra-large sinks and drying racks for clothes, four normal sinks for washing up, and a row of toilet stalls without doors. I took a pee like I'd never peed before. Relieved but with exhaustion catching up to me, I fumbled into the clothes Mrs. Anders had handed over: a calf-length jeans skirt with an already stretched out maternity panel, a bleach-speckled navy-blue turtleneck, and a heavy cream-colored cardigan sweater. All had seen heavy wear and were too large for me by a size or more.

I kept my undies, socks, and Sketchers, since no replacements had been offered.

"There now. You look real sweet." Mrs. Anders said when I emerged in the "new" outfit.

The old lady gave me her first smile since she'd presented herself back at the big house. Her face didn't crack, after all. It looked like Jo Beth had managed to chat her up a bit. A chummy air prevailed between the two of them.

Mrs. Anders tucked my rolled-up jeans and sweatshirt under her arm.

She said, "I'll let you and Sis say yer good-byes now." And with a nod to Jo Beth, "When I pull my black Bronco up that gravel drive, I'm ready to run you back to town. I'll blow the horn so you know I'm there. But no rush."

I felt embarrassed for Jo Beth to see me in that get-up: skirt that reached the tops of my socks and sleeves covering half my hands, although soon enough, I would appreciate the extra inch of warmth. She didn't waste a breath teasing me, though. Just put her hands on my shoulders and gave me a deep look in the eyes.

"So, listen. That old gal says they'll crank up the heat before you all come in here to get ready for bed. That's the good news. And she says not to worry—nobody's allowed to pick on you so long as you walk the straight and narrow. Just don't break any rules. Not one! They watch like hawks. Nobody gets away with a single thing."

She dropped to the hoarse whisper she'd used on the bus. "And don't fret about the baby. Momma's got a brilliant idea for how we can handle things. She's gonna write and explain everything. We'll all write to you."

There was no reason for this advice to sound daunting. I was known for being the kid who never called down punishment. So maybe it was just the realization that the last familiar face in my life was minutes from going away, leaving me in this cold place, that forced the tears out my eyes and down my cheeks. Jo Beth gathered me into a big hug and rocked me side to side. When she held me out to arms length again, I saw her eyes had teared up, too.

"Time will fly," she promised. With wonder, I heard a slight catch in her voice. "You'll be back home before you know it."

That was the one true blessing of my entire time in Missouri: I got to see in that moment, plain as day, that my sister really did care for me. But Jo Beth was wrong about how things would happen—I wouldn't go home before I knew it. My baby was due in five months. Springtime. But I wound up staying at New Dawn Ministry until the next fall.

Our schooling was held in the dining hall and the non-bunk area of the dormitories. Education consisted of Bible study, which covered English, history, and civics. Then there was arithmetic and home economics, which doubled as kitchen duty. Physical Education consisted of running (or for pregnant girls, walking) a circuit around the campus for 45 minutes, twice each day. I would later learn that The Ministry had a website on which it was claimed that, "Our young ladies prepare to pass the GED exam, and even score highly on SATs."

You could not have proved it from the classes I experienced.

The four pillars that Headmistress Fitzsimmons had spoken about were ever-present. The pillar of prayer consisted of half an hour on our knees in the bunkhouse morning and evening, plus service in the chapel six days a week and three hours on Sunday. The service pillar meant two hours of cleaning every day except Sunday, plus rotating kitchen duty. Additional service duties could be imposed under punishment conditions. Reflection was limited to three hours on Sunday afternoons when we were expected to write letters home or read books from the ministry library. I guess reflection also included guided discussions of religious films that were viewed in the dining hall two or more evenings per week.

All of the above activities, pursued in strictly ordered fashion day after day, made up the pillar of discipline. It covered every minute of our time.

Supervision was provided by a crew of older girls around Jo Beth's age. They were known as "elders." Most were recent graduates of The Program. Presumably, they had overcome the problems that landed them here to begin with. They now earned some small wage for living in our midst, watching every move, and eavesdropping on the younger, as yet imperfectly corrected, population. Three to five elders were assigned to each bunkhouse at all times. They were easy to distinguish from the likes of us by their uniforms of khaki cargo pants and dark-colored sweatshirts. Their clothing was newer than ours and better fitted. They also had puffy hooded coats for outdoor supervision, while we relied for warmth on layers of knit tops, sweatshirts, and physical exertion.

Then there was a group of local women known as trustees, like Mrs. Anders, who oversaw transportation and deliveries, supervised our work duty, read and corrected all letters home, and the like. A special sub-group were cooks and supervisors of kitchen duty. Trustees commuted to work at The Ministry from neighboring farms. Also, there were three or four class-room teachers, whose number was sometimes supplemented by Mr. or Mrs. Fitzsimmons. The latter lived in the big house full-time, while the credentialed teachers drove out from Rich Hill or other towns several times per week.

When I arrived, there were about forty girls in residence. Other times during my stay, there were as many as sixty or as few as thirty. We were required to get out of bed at five o'clock every morning and lie down at nine-thirty every night. We had to clean our plates at all meals, do our work "with energy and good cheer," wear only assigned clothing at all times, with hair in a single braid or low ponytail. Those who arrived with hair too short for the approved styles wore blue bandana headscarves until it grew out sufficiently.

We were not allowed to get packages; to have money, sweets, jewelry, cosmetics, or unapproved reading matter; to watch TV or hear radio other than pre-selected programs that were viewed in groups. We were especially not allowed to chat idly with each other, speak without permission, talk back to elders, look anyone in the eye unless so instructed, heave sighs, turn our backs, or otherwise show disrespect.

Many forms of correction were available to help us follow these rules and prohibitions. All elders were empowered to carry a length of 1-inch PVC pipe to administer correction, primarily to our hands, arms, legs, or shoulders. The top or back of the head might also be a target. I believe they were instructed to spare our faces because a few girls had family who came for visits on Sundays. Trustees rarely wielded pipes and some declined to carry them at all, but the elders relied on them keenly.

Among the girls, PVC was short for "Positively Very Cruel."

As days and weeks passed, I would learn about other punishments that could be handed down only by trustees or the headmistress herself. By contrast, girls said that Headmaster Fitzsimmons did not administer or assign any punishments at all.

His job was granting rewards.

I came to the Ministry on a Wednesday and, after Jo Beth's departure, received the special attention of an elder named Blake. Elders were addressed by last name only. Blake was tall and thick around the middle with red-brown hair in a long straight ponytail. She maintained an evenly grave face, sneering ever so slightly at my early attempt at a smile, but she didn't seem actively mean. Not at first, anyway. She came to collect me at the bunkhouse, pointed out two empty drawers for my assigned clothing and gave a rundown on basic "behavioral expectations," while watching me make up my bunk. Then she walked me to the dining hall where several dozen girls were already sitting or bringing their trays to the long tables, most with a trustee at the head.

I saw that all the girls' clothes lined up in a color scheme of blues, browns, yellows, and shades of white. There was nothing in the red range, nor darker than navy. Nothing brighter than the occasional royal-blue bandana. Here and there, I spotted a sweater that might qualify as lavender. Nothing orange, nor even pink.

Only a few girls glanced up in my direction. In silence, Blake pointed out where I should go. It gave me a bad feeling that there was no talking during the meal, but I was glad enough to focus on filling my stomach, which had become increasingly demanding since I'd left Ohio. I was given something the gray-haired woman at the steam table called a "special ration." Blake directed me to a table with five other girls who had the same. So far as I could tell, we each got a small hamburger patty in addition to the mac'n'cheese, bread roll, and green beans that everybody else got. There was also a cup of fruit cocktail and a mini milk carton.

Soon enough, I would understand that the extras were for pregnant girls.

The food was not bad, but it would quickly become monotonous. There were only three or four rotating dishes for each meal.

Blake sat beside me and reminded everyone at the table, "Eyes on your plates. Don't slouch. Don't clang with your spoon."

After lunch, we all went to chapel. As a newcomer, I was instructed to kneel on a step below the altar where I would serve as an object of special prayer. This was my first introduction to Headmaster Fitzsimmons. He was a square-faced man of about sixty with abundant white hair that curled into a little flip at the base of his neck. Medium height but built like a brick, he wore a dark suit with a white shirt and red-and-white striped tie. Aside from a different tie or two, this was the only outfit I ever saw on him.

Once everyone was assembled, from us lowly girls to elders, trustees, and teachers, Mr. Fitzsimmons came to stand before me and moved his hands over my head and shoulders

as if to cover me with a close-fitting, invisible cup. His boom-
ing voice issued a heartfelt appeal.

"Gracious Lord, help this troubled lamb receive Your
healing balm of which she stands in such great need. Let our
ministry family demonstrate to her the eternal love that flows
from Your Son, our Lord and Savior Jesus Christ—"

As a building that only saw use for one hour most days of
the week, the chapel was heated only a short time before we
entered and for so long as the service continued. It felt very
cold. I was relieved, and somewhat warmed, when my special
prayer ended and Blake pointed me toward a pew where I sat
among the other girls for songs and readings.

From there, we walked to the big house and Blake put me
to work dusting and sweeping the downstairs. There was a
large foyer across the hallway from the old-fashioned parlor,
and behind those, a nice library room. All had high ceilings,
pretty lamps and thick rugs. The walls were hung with pictures of old-fashioned farm scenes. I liked the one of a tabby
cat riding on a big draft horse's rump, led on a halter rope by
a barefoot boy in overalls.

"Don't gawk," Blake said. "Work."

She hit me a sharp blow with the 15-inch stick of PVC
pipe. The one she carried was fitted with a three-way joint
that left red half-moons on my wrist. I gasped from surprise
almost more than from pain—she whipped that thing out
and struck so fast, with no warning.

Of course, I didn't cry or complain. Just gave her a big-
eyed stare for one second before looking down to the dustpile
my sweeping had gathered.

She bestowed a word of explanation. "You're lucky to be
in the house, here. It's way better than scrubbing bathrooms,
breathing that full-strength bleach."

Also, as I would learn, the big house was by far the

warmest place in the compound. That and the dining hall, once the kitchen got fired up.

"Yeah, you're getting off easy," Blake went on. "But it ain't for your own sake. It's light duty for the baby. So don't get a big head."

Maybe Blake was disappointed that I wasn't a backtalker, nor a slacker, nor malingerer. I gave her precious few openings to strike. The only other time was that evening during the half-hour kneel before bed. All the girls were down, praying between the bunks, and elders were on the prowl with their pipes, smacking anybody who sat back on her heels or mumbled gibberish instead of proper words of contrition. At one point, about halfway through, I stretched my neck to one side to relieve my shoulder.

There was Blake. She knocked me a hard one smack on top of my head.

"Keep still," she said. "Pray right."

After that, I guess I was considered fully oriented to the Program of the Four Pillars. The next morning, I joined a classroom that met one bunkhouse over. Memorizing Bible verses and writing two pages on my need for God's grace, were not terribly hard assignments for me. I gathered that a couple of girls in the class could barely read or spell, so they drew the punishments—mainly standing with their noses in a circle on the wall, drawn just a bit too high to reach flatfooted. Then it was kitchen duty, lunch, chapel, math class, work duty, Phys. Ed., dinner, a movie and discussion. The movie concerned the Rapture and Satan's dreaded 1000-year reign.

On Friday, a special occasion rolled around known as "Social Hour." I had come to understand that this was a much longed-for time among the girls in my bunkhouse. It was the only time when girls were permitted to talk, more or less freely, amongst ourselves outside of duty-related communication.

Naturally, elders circulated around the room to eavesdrop. We received popcorn and fruit punch for the occasion.

Again, I was presented as a new lost lamb—this time, by a trustee named Mrs. Lemoyne. Singled out this way, I became the focus for a dozen or more girls to make a beeline and talk my ear off. Most, I figured, were brown-nosers showing off for Mrs. Lemoyne's good graces. They heaped praise on all the help we were getting to live in righteousness. A few did offer helpful advice: "When you hang your underthings to dry in the washroom, it's a smart idea to safety-pin all your stuff together, so nothing goes missing." And, "When we have Phys. Ed. outside, put on extra tops under your sweatshirt. That wind is something fierce!"

One girl with a blond braid whispered, "They'll still give you pads even though you're pregnant. Give your extra pads to me, please?"

Remember, this was the best chance a crowd of teenage girls would have to communicate for another whole week. Over time, I heard a lot of crazy stuff murmured in quiet, pleasant tones so the lurking elders wouldn't catch on.

But that first week, I was so exhausted, I just tried to keep a halfway attentive look on my face and let the talkers talk. As their words babbled past me, my mind found a quiet corner where a few thoughts came through from my former life. Mostly, it was Jo Beth's announcements that came back to me.

Jay's a grown man. He can marry me. ... This is not my first ... he took me to Columbus to the Choice Clinic.

So—let's get this straight: My sister was just as careless as me, but she went and turned back the clock. Got an abortion. A do-over. Tra-la, no show, no sin! Start fresh and no one the wiser! Oops, knocked up again? Get married this time. Get out from under Dad's thumb!

All this felt like a scared-crazy cat trying to claw its way out of my heart. So—if I hadn't been deluded about Bernard still loving me (or loving me in the first place), I could of got my ass up to Columbus in time, and turned back the clock at some secret clinic. I could of stayed in school, stayed home, nobody knowing a thing, and I wouldn't of made my parents ashamed of me?

And what did Jo Beth mean by *Momma's got a big idea for how we can handle the baby—?* I know it's hard for an adult to believe, but being pregnant had gotten so overwhelming, in and of itself, that I hadn't spared an inkling for how to "handle the baby." Huge heap of diapers and bottles of milk, I figured. There, my thinking on the matter pretty much came to a halt.

By the time Mrs. Lemoyne flicked the lights off and on a few times—the signal to quiet down and get ready for prayers, chop-chop—a heavy feeling had settled into my body. I saw pictures in my mind of men on chain gangs in the Old South limping along with a shuffle and drag. The heft of an iron ball, big as my head, held me down by a clanking chain clamped to my foot. Down, down—flat on the earth as a lifeless tarp.

After a couple of minutes on my knees, I swayed side to side and had to catch myself with both hands on the floor. Blake was still hovering near me. But this this time, she tapped me with her PVC, just gently, and permitted me to finish prayers sitting on my bunk.

Throwing up in the mornings had not been a major problem for me, although the nausea could hit sporadically at other times. But by the end of January, I started getting heartburn something terrible, especially right after breakfast. I'd never had it before—such nastiness at the back of my throat!

One of the older girls explained, "It's the orange juice. Same with vinegar dressing and stuff like that. You know, 'acid reflux'?"

That made sense from how it came on, but there wasn't a lot I could do about it. Pregnant or not, we weren't allowed to refuse anything we were supposed to eat. The attempt could get you locked in an unheated closet with more of the offending item, until you relented and choked it down.

So this older girl (I think her name was Janice, but we didn't get to be friends—she had her baby and went home about a week later), she taught me some tricks: How to spill juice and dilute the remainder with water. Never too much spillage in one place: a little on the tray, little on the floor, a drop on the table, a splash in the trash. Or sometimes, you could slip all or some of your juice to one of the non-pregnant girls—the great majority of our population.

Most of them would gladly down it ASAP. They didn't get real juice. Only some kind of red or orange Tang.

Also, it was hard for me to go through a full day without extra sleep. In principle, pregnant girls could request a break part way through work duty for a bathroom visit or short rest. But that first week, while I was still learning the routines, I saw one girl smacked by two elders at once for taking a lie-down in the middle of sweeping the bunkhouse. Maybe she had forgot to ask for authorization.

She screamed at the elders, "Lay off, you bitches—I'm pregnant," which landed her with another half-dozen smacks. They were going to lock her in a closet, too, but Mrs. Walters stepped in and let her apologize, instead.

So I muddled along as best I could. Usually, I managed to eat fast enough that I'd could fit in a catnap between lunch and chapel.

On my second Sunday at The Ministry, during Reflection, Mrs. Anders handed me a small pile of mail from home. The dining hall tables had been cleared and wiped down, and a murmur of excitement floated on the air as girls read through their haul of mail. I got a "Thinking of You" card from Jo Beth with calico kittens in a basket and a couple of Marietta postcards—one from Effie and one from Aunt Sue. And there was a letter from Momma. At first, when I saw these and started reading, I felt myself gearing up for a big cry.

But that stopped as I worked my way through the letter.

LaDene, my darling girl,

It's eight days now that you've been away from our home, so far away at The Missouri Ministry. Daddy and I both miss you very much and we think of you every day and hold you in our prayers. We hope you are making new friends and keeping a positive outlook. We will be overjoyed to see you back in our home very soon. It may seem a long time, but it will surely pass in a twinkling.

Remember that we all love you no matter what.

Your daddy has spoken on the telephone with Mr. and Mrs. Fitzsimmons, your Headmasters over there. They have told us that you are adjusting well to The Ministry Program. You are a good girl who has a sweet nature and seeks the righteous path, Mrs. Fitzsimmons says. She praised your schoolwork and your work ethic and good attitude. Of course, I know she is right about all of this because you always have been my good sweet daughter. Your one mistake will not leave a black mark against you forever, you can be sure of that.

Effie was home for Sunday dinner this past week and she sends you her love and all best hopes for the weeks flying by. She has gotten a promotion at the IGA and is now assistant bakery manager. She brought us a German chocolate cake and has everyone putting on the pounds. Ha-ha! She and Nathan are doing good, getting along as usual, but have still not set any wedding plans.

But as you know, Jo Beth is getting married this Friday to Jay McLaughlin at the Wood County Courthouse over in Parkersburg. Daddy had a long talk with Jay, and we all agree that he's got the makings of a good husband. Jo Beth says she did not discuss with you our idea for the "next generation." Even though she has left it to me to explain things, you can have fullest confidence that she is on board and will do everything for the good of our family.

Here is what we think—

The way I calculate, you are no more than 6-7 weeks further along than she is. That is not such a lot that we cannot let the babies grow up as twins. Jo Beth will be married, and we don't have to "show off" until they have a chance to catch up in size and weight. We can always say that one of them had the jaundice, but really who is going to ask? It is no one's business but our own. Jo Beth will be a good mother, and the father will be working steady to provide. Jay has applied for a county job or may even get on at Guarantee. His dad is going to the Riverside Care Home soon and will leave his house in Lower Salem for them. So it will be a nice home and stable environment.

You must understand that your daddy and I would not be able to provide such a nice family atmosphere to you and baby.

Rest assured, darling, that you will always be the "Favorite Auntie" and will be able to play a very important part in the child's life. When you finish school and have a chance to grow up, it will be time for you to have your own family. Your little niece or nephew by sister Jo Beth can still be a special person to you.

We all agree that this is for the best.

I am so anxious to hear from you and how you are feeling. Homesickness is to be expected but count off the days and keep us posted. Write home soon and let me know what you think and how you are getting along.

With love always,

Your Momma

THE LETTER AND CARD had both been opened before the trustee presented them to me. I wondered if Momma knew this would happen, that her plans for a secret family arrangement would be common knowledge to Mrs. Anders, the Fitzsimmonses, and whoever happened to slice the envelope, or just strolled by at the time. I wondered what she meant by me letting her "know what I thought." It sounded like an invitation to share my own view of the plan, but then again, precious little room appeared for a difference of opinion.

Instead of the homesick tears I'd been ready to shed, my stomach clenched like a fist. I felt the surge of lunch rise to my throat. There wasn't time to get to a bathroom. Pictures in my head of Very Cruel pipes raining down kept me from turning to the open floor beside my seat in the dining hall. So I puked into my skirt. Bent forward, I laid the side of my head on the table and gathered wet fabric up into my lap.

Mrs. Anders gave me permission to spend the rest of Reflection Time on my bunk.

Such a relief that was. Sunrays came in the windows on the opposite wall as I snuggled under my blanket in a warm nightgown. The whole dormitory was quiet, all to myself. That's when it came to me that the baby I'd conceived was a person who would have a real life in this world, once he or she came outside of me. It wasn't just "me being pregnant." It was a whole new human coming into the trials and tribulation we all drag in our wake.

I pictured the surge of the Muskingum River pouring over Devola Dam at flood stage—scary and unstoppable. Huge cottonwood logs could get swept away on that water, like I was swept along by everything that had happened. That was the power of the baby growing inside me. It had uprooted my life.

It helped me relax to picture the river, give in to the current. But from there, I couldn't see anything else. No people on the banks, no nostalgic views of Devola. Everything just went blank, like my mind had no further ideas. So I pulled cold air into my nostrils till I dropped like a stone into a deep, empty sleep for the rest of the afternoon.

* * *

INSTEAD OF RUNNING AROUND the compound before breakfast and dinner, us pregnant girls walked for our Phys. Ed. We might've preferred jogging for the sake of warmth, but that was not allowed. So we linked arms and huddled up and walked like a crosswise centipede.

Usually, Mrs. Virland was the trustee who walked with us. She was by far the kindest of the trustees, so far as I ever saw, and as such she was widely beloved. Nearly a 200-pounder and not much over five feet tall, she said it was good for her health to walk with us. So long as we didn't move any faster than she could keep up with, she swore no harm would come to our babies. She talked a lot about babies, of which she herself had birthed five, and she sometimes let us voice our fears of the dire pains and torn flesh that awaited us.

"None of that, now!" she'd say, but in a comforting manner. "The Blessed Mother holds birthing women in her own two hands. She keeps all harm at bay!"

At first I didn't understand that by this she meant the Virgin Mary, who would serve as our special guardian when our labors began. Later on, a bunkmate told me, "Old lady Virland is of the Catholic persuasion. But we don't rat on her."

When she got to huffing and puffing on our second or third lap round the buildings, Mrs. Virland would push the hood of her parka off her head and say, "Hoo, girls! Let's slow it down just a tad, now."

She had small cheerful eyes and string-straight iron-gray hair that she wore, like us, in a blunt ponytail at the nape of her neck. With nothing but headscarves and sweatshirts, under which we wore any T-shirts or turtlenecks we could find, most of us tried to gradually push the pace up faster again.

Of course, the numbers of pregnant girls could undergo rapid change. Three gave birth ahead of me during my months of waiting. Each of them vanished abruptly—on one occasion, in the middle of chapel—never to reappear.

"Years back, we had a lot more of you young moms here at The New Dawn," Mrs. Virland would remark, from time to time. She tended to repeat herself. "Nowadays, all's we get are these deviants and drug addicts. Not so many 'fallen women,' like we used to call you'uns. More of 'em just stay home now, I s'pose. That's all right. Families are standing by you. That's the good way."

All of us were nervous over what would become of us, family standing by, or not. Where would we be whisked off to when our time was at hand? What could we expect? A visiting nurse drove out from Butler every week or so to check our blood pressure and such, but she was famously tight-mouthed, offering not much in the way of advice or encouragement.

"Mr. or Mrs. Fitzsimmons will take you to Bates County Hospital. Or I'll take you myself, if they cain't for whichever reason. Have no fear! Bates has good doctors and all the up-to-date instruments you need. Not like we had back in my day!"

We begged to hear what Mrs. Virland had suffered in her day.

"Lordy! I labored two solid days with my first. First one is bound to be the hardest, especially if it's a boy. Boys don't like to leave their mommas. I very nearly begged the Lord to take me now and end it all. But finally, out come my Roger, feet first. Eight and three-quarter pounds! Like to kilt me. But don't you fret, girls. Our Blessed Mother holds women in her own two hands."

One February afternoon, when there were six of us in the pregnant cohort, weather had shifted from cold to almost balmy. Gray ribs of whalebone clouds blanketed most of the sky. Mrs. Virland paused in our circuit by the backstretch of fencing where the dining hall blocked all view from the other buildings except the attic window of the big house. She dragged her feet till we all came to a full stop.

"Whoa, girls. Take a breather," the trustee said. Then, raising a hand to her forehead, "Why, what's that I see off yonder? Like a dust devil blowing o'er the field—"

We stopped and looked. Sure enough, a green tractor appeared to be plowing our way over the cornrows, raising a light trail of dust.

The senior girls among us let out shrieks of delight.

"Is that him?" one asked.

"Is it Mr. Virland?"

We had heard that, once a blue moon, the old couple would engineer a minor miracle for our unworthy benefit.

Indeed, as Mrs. Virland evaded our questions, the John Deere rolled to a stop some twenty feet shy of where we stood. A lean old man in tan cap and coveralls swung open the door of his little cab and climbed out. On long strides, he crossed the remaining space toward us.

Several called out to him, and everyone chattered at once.

"Keep it down, girls. Fitzsimmons ain't deaf, ya know," our trustee chided.

Her husband came up to the fence, a broad grin across his furrowed face. He held up a brown paper bag, gave it a slight shake as if listening for telltale sounds from inside. With a couple steps back and a dramatic windup, he made one long, high toss over the barbwire.

The package landed behind us on brown grass with a crisp *smack!* All us girls ran to fetch it.

"Don't anybody open it, now," Mrs. Virland said. "You just bring it right to me."

Of course we obeyed.

When we surrendered the bag, she pulled apart several staples at the top end and explained, "I forgot my lunch this morning, don't ya know. Mister had to bring it to me for my special diet. I cain't eat that slop you'uns get. I mean, all those beans and starch." She pulled a checkered tea towel from the bag. "Why look here! He brung us a little something extra—"

Inside the towel, inside a square Tupperware, there were two stacks of large chocolate brownies, exactly enough for each of us girls to have one. Again, we shrieked with delight.

"Here you go. Here you go," Mrs. Virland handed round the treats. "Don't bolt it down, now. Easy does it."

The bittersweet scent was overpowering. We inhaled those brownies, licked our fingertips, sucked in our cheeks to extract every morsel of flavor. It was the strongest drug ever to exist. I'm sure I speak for all in saying, we had never tasted anything so delicious.

"Remember, girls, if anybody asks, my hubby just tossed my lunch over to me. You got it?"

We all promised we got it.

"Tell Mr. Virland bye-bye, now." She raised a hand and called to him, "Thank you, Sweet Pie."

I was feeling so uplifted from the sugar rush and the special moment, so moved beyond the ordinary, I repeated her exact words.

"Thank you, Sweet Pie!" I called out.

A black-haired girl from my bunkhouse—Sarah was her name—hit me a hard slug on the shoulder. "Dipshit!" she said. "You don't call her husband 'Sweet Pie'. Only Mrs. V. calls him that!"

A fat girl whose name I never learned also piled on and hit me on the ear, which hurt something fierce.

But Mr. Virland was grinning bigger than ever. He appeared in no rush to head back to his John Deere.

And Mrs. Virland said, "Don't be hitting her, you ruffians. Aren't you'uns all in the same old boat?" She was chuckling under her breath as she waved to her husband again and began walking slowly forward, back to our circuit.

"That's all right, dearies," I heard her say. "She give that old man the biggest thrill he's had in years."

Some weeks later, I learned that Sarah made the mistake of trying to get a much bigger favor out of Mrs. Virland. She should of known better. Even I could figure it was insane to ask a trustee to mail an uncensored letter, in which she begged to go back home, claiming she'd been beaten black and blue by "girl thugs" with lengths of PVC pipe.

Sarah had to know that "contraband mailings" were among the most forbidden acts at The Ministry. No way was Mrs. Virland going to join in such a deed. Worse yet, as later heard from the grapevine, Sarah didn't just plead for help, knowing that the Virlands were kindly souls. She attempted blackmail, threatening to tell Mr. Fitzsimmons about the brownie toss. Sarah (allegedly) assumed this would frighten our benefactress, on pain of losing her job as trustee.

But in fact, the result was Sarah getting beaten by a crew of four elders, only somewhat merciful due to her being pregnant. The "black and blue" part came true in spades, all over her shins and forearms.

*You don't talk about trustees. You don't carry tales. You
don't send secret letters. Huh-uh. Not the likes of you.*

That's the kind of thing they yelled while they beat her.
She screamed and swore she'd never do it again. I heard that
part firsthand, because I was doing laundry in the washroom
when it happened. But also, I heard later from a girl named
Annalee that Mrs. Virland was the last person to fear losing
her job at The Ministry.

"Think about it," Annalee said. "The Virlands own all the
farmland around this place. Fitzsimmons needs them more
than they need him. He lands on their bad side, they could decide to help escapees, not just hand out treats when it suits 'em."

Annalee was someone I came to trust more than most.

* * *

ON SUNDAYS, WE USUALLY GOT A DISH of canned peaches or
pears with the noon dinner. On Easter, apple crisp was
served (no whip cream, though). But other than Mrs.
Virland, the only person who ever offered chocolate was
the headmaster himself.

As you would expect, rumors concerning the headmaster and mistress were wild and numerous. Opportunities to
gossip were scarce, but those two topped the list with tales of
their past escapades in juvenile rehabilitation. I expect some
contained grains of truth. Nearly all seemed believable based
on general observation.

It was said that Mr. Fitzsimmons' job history was mainly
in the automotive trades. He was not a registered minister of
any church. He had served jail time for breaking the collarbone of a boy he disciplined at a rehab ranch in Texas. He
also, supposedly, shot a man that attempted to steal a car
from the sales lot where he worked in Oklahoma. And he
may have killed another in a shooting at a church parking lot,

but that victim definitely deserved it, in fact he was a suspect-
ed serial killer who'd claimed the lives of numerous college
girls and prostitutes along the Gulf Coast.

Fitzsimmons was alleged to have a previous wife, a social
worker from Abilene, who got him started in the family-in-
tervention business. That first wife, however, balked at the
extensive use of corporal punishment required for convincing
recalcitrant boys to embrace obedience. Worse yet, she had
no head for making money.

By contrast, the current Mrs. Fitzsimmons had run a
cleaning service, or maybe a bowling alley, as well as own-
ing a chain of beauty salons, over the course of her three
earlier marriages, one of which may have ended with the husband's suspicious death by electrocution while attempting to
repair a washing machine in the basement of the home. It was
also claimed that our headmistress had been a stripper in San
Antonio, a whorehouse madam in Reno, hostess at a poker
room in Atlantic City, and many other things in many places.

Several girls attested that she took a vacation to Kansas City
after Christmas and spent much of her time thrift-store shopping
for the drab clothes we all wore. Everything personally selected.

When this born manager landed the job as director of
outreach and recruitment at the Texas boys' ranch, she recognized Mr. Fitzsimmons' talents, and quickly sent the mousy
first wife packing. When her new hubby was charged with
child abuse, after a string of incriminating injuries, she was
credited with shredding records, selling off supplies, ship-
ping boys home in the middle of the night, and closing down
the facility like it had never existed. After Mr. Fitzsimmons
served his time (three months? three years?), they came to
Missouri and started their very own ministry, which had also
changed locations once or twice before settling on a corner of
the Virland farm outside Rich Hill.

"Girls are better to work with than boys. So much easier to control. Not because of physical weakness. It's their emotional nature that gives you a mighty lever," Mr. Fitz was alleged to have told a group of trustees, within hearing of a girl on work duty in the big house.

My greater impression of the headmaster began one afternoon in late February, when I got sent to the big house with a group of a dozen girls for what was billed as a "fatherly chat." Girls were called from different bunkhouses for these occasions, mostly during math class. As we crunched our way across the gravel drive, one girl fell in step with me and spoke in a real quiet voice.

"You're over here a lot, right? You clean the parlor and all?"

"Sometimes," I said.

This was about six weeks into my time away from home, and I was still wary when some girl would up and talk to me out of the blue. Made me suspicious. I'd seen that some would try to draw others out just for the thrill, or the brownie points, of reporting you to an elder for "idle talk." Over time, I would develop a better sense of who was gaming and who had a true reason for wanting someone to talk to.

"If you ever clean the bathroom off the library," this girl said, "there's a box of tissues on the toilet tank? Real soft—top dollar. Put a few in your pocket, bring them to chapel. I'll make it worth your while."

Lots of girls had sniffles, and there were complaints about the awful toilet paper in the bunkhouses—miserable on raw nostrils. And that paper was rationed, anyways.

"Just, you know, if you get a chance," the girl said.

I glanced her way, saw that she was a chunky girl with the kind of chalk-white skin that flushes easy. Right then her cheeks were red in the wind. Under a bandana, her white-blond hair was full and frizzy, not quite long enough to pull into a ponytail.

But she had the confidence of one who knew the ropes, so her hair must of been super-short when she first arrived.

She didn't look at me, but added, "I'm Annalee Blanchard from Jeff County, outside St. Louis. I'm not a rat or anything."

"I'm not a rat, either. LaDene from Devola, Ohio."

"Good deal, LaDene."

Our group came up to the porch steps of the big house, and everyone fell silent. An elder named Maxwell, who'd herded us over from class, led us inside toward the staircase amid instructions: "Hands to yourselves. Grubby fingers off the wall! Step light, not like cattle—the heads are busy working here."

In the second-floor office, Mr. Fitzsimmons was standing by a shelf next to a dark wooden desk under a large bare cross that hung on the striped wallpaper. When the first of us approached the doorway, he looked up from a book in his hand with an expression of happy surprise, as if he hadn't heard us clomping like cattle at all. He clapped the book shut, set it on the corner of the desk, and stepped out onto a green rug with paisley patterns. As we bunched up just inside the door, he spread his arms wide, like he often did in chapel, and bestowed a grand smile.

"Come in, girls. Come right in." His arms swept toward the folding chairs set in a circle around the rug. "Take a seat. I want to get to know you. Don't be shy—take any chair."

I managed to sit next to Annalee. She seemed a good person to know. All the folding chairs filled up. The elder, Maxwell, stationed herself by the door behind us.

A shaft of sunlight brightened the west-facing windows, then dimmed again behind fast-moving clouds. The headmaster sat on an upholstered chair at the top of the group, out front of his desk.

"Isn't this nice?" His eyes ran round us. His smile widened. "It is so good to get to see you girls, here in a homey setting.

Tell me, how many of you have been to one of our fatherly chats before?"

Two girls raised their hands, including Annalee.

A third spoke up, saying, "I have, too, Mr. Fitzsimmons."

Annalee would tell me later that most girls wound up going to chats about once a season, up to four times, if they stayed a full year, which sounded like eternity. The way it worked was, they called us up at a time when we'd had no recent infractions.

"So it's like a big privilege," Annalee said.

"Good. Excellent," the headmaster went on. "I'm so happy to see you girls again. And to meet all you new girls, up close and personal."

His eyes rested on each of us, one at a time, with a kindly glint. If possible, his smile seemed to grow warmer with each new face he turned to. It occurs to me now, that must be a special skill few can master.

"Now, why don't we go round the circle and each of you say your name. Your full first name, so I can start to learn."

At the headmaster's nod, we started to speak—*Molly, Destiny, Rachel, Jeanine, Emily, Kylie, Shawndra, Tiffany, Sophia, Teresa, Annalee, LaDene...*

"Lovely, girls! Your names and your voices are like music. Music to my ears!"

I didn't know if we were permitted to look across the group at each other, which could involve eye contact—normally a big no-no—so I must of been glancing all around like a trapped animal.

"Don't be nervous—LaDene, was it?" the headmaster said.

Singled out! I wanted to drop through the floor. I didn't know if it was permitted to look at him, so I kept my eyes on my hands in my lap and didn't answer.

"This is our special time." The Headmaster leaned in my

general direction but spoke to the group. "There's no wrong answers, no trick questions here. Just a nice little talk, like in your own dear families, back at home."

He ran a hand through his wavy white hair, clapped palms on his thighs, and rose from his seat. He stepped to a corner of the room and brought a square card table to the center of the circle. Unfolding the four legs, he set it upright. This kind of reminded me of watching a magician set up his act, like draping a magic tablecloth over his assistant.

I could feel Annalee's leg start to jostle beside me as her heel went up and down at a furious pace. She kept her head bowed and didn't make a sound.

"Now!" Mr. Fitzsimmons exclaimed. "You girls who know about this, don't spoil the surprise."

He surveyed us again with the kindly, but now a mite mischievous, smile. Then he stepped back to his desk and fetched something that rustled like plastic from a squeaky drawer.

As he returned, I saw that it was a bag of mini-Mars bars, the "fun size" like you might give out on Halloween—good for two bites if you stretched it.

He paused by the card table and gave a small lecture.

"Girls, my dear sweet girls, one of the crucial tasks every human being must accomplish on this earth is to learn an essential ability known as *self-control*. It is the key to right living, right attitude, and the state of sacred grace for which we all strive. Think on that, girls. *Self-control* is your key to *freedom from sin*."

He was warming up to his chapel-preaching voice. The elevated volume made my hands feel shaky. I gripped them in my lap.

"Now, all of you girls have struggled with self-control in the past. I know you've struggled. You all know you've struggled. It is no secret."

He put up his hands, gave us the one-by-one look, but this time without any smile.

"As it's written in the book of Timothy: 'Women should adorn themselves with modesty and *self-control.*' So as part of our get-together today, we are going to practice your self-control."

He ripped open the bag of candy and rustled through the Mars bars as he grasped a goodly handful. He held them over the table for a second, then dropped the candies to its surface.

They bounced, rolled, and fell still.

"Which of you has been to our chats before—Molly and Rachel? You come up here and count out one dozen chocolate bars for the one dozen girls we've got here in this room."

The two from my bunkhouse got up and did as he said. They scooped the extras to one side and returned to their seats.

"Now. You—Miss Annalee—you come place that dozen in a circle on the table, just like we are sitting here."

Annalee's heel froze its jostling. She did as he told her, but she didn't sit back down. I had raised my eyes to observe and was surprised to see Annalee pause and wait by the table, at attention. She even looked up at Mr. Fitzsimmons and arched her eyebrows, ever so slightly.

"Now, Annalee, you put those leftover chocolates back in this bag."

He held out the bag, and she dropped the excess three or four pieces into it. He gave a slight nod, and she returned to the seat beside me, where she recommenced to shaking her foot.

"Very good."

The headmaster tossed the candy bag onto his desk and returned to sit among us in his upholstered chair.

"Now! What we are going to do is, we'll go round this circle and take turns sharing one small success from your recent time here at New Dawn Ministry. Each of you can tell us something. Perhaps you felt the spark of God's joy while doing your work in the kitchen this morning, helping provide a meal for your sisters in Christ. Or at chapel this noon, perhaps you felt the relief of true repentance for one of your sins."

His open palm seemed to demonstrate how easy and wonderful it would be for us to speak, in front of everyone, about such things.

"And then, girls—" here he raised an instructive finger— "those of you who've chatted with me before most likely remember, after you've shared your sweet story of success with us all, you may approach the table here." His hand roved toward the treats arranged in a circle. "Come forward, open the wrapper on the chocolate bar nearest to you, and—what next? Molly?"

He turned to the girl who'd boasted she had attended chat before.

Molly said, "We'll unwrap the chocolate, take a good look, and set it right back down on the table."

"Good, good. That's right. You'll take a look. Take a sniff. And set it *right back on the table*." Mr. Fitzsimmons chuckled. "An eyeful, but not a mouthful! Miss Molly, why don't you show us how it's done."

Molly's dark eyes darted around the room. A raw-boned, skinny girl, she clasped and raised her hands, like she was about to recite a prayer. She said, "I awoke this morning with a light heart and a happy mood. God has taken away my depression. Thanks be to God."

I picked up the cue from those around me and joined in repeating, "Thanks be to God."

Molly looked to the headmaster and waited for his nod before she went to the table. She picked up and unwrapped a Mars bar, held it close to her face for a second, then set it back down and returned to her seat.

Mr. Fitzsimmons looked to the girl on Molly's right. "Destiny?" he said.

The process continued. Some girls giggled, shrugged, hesitated. The "father" of our fatherly chat insisted in a patient voice that we could surely think of something good that the Lord had blessed us with lately.

The voices were like a call and response, with "Thanks be to God" after each girl's statement—

I heard somebody complain about eggs at breakfast. I just prayed for her ... During Phys. Ed., we saw a redbird on the fence, and we all thanked God for it ... I prayed for the woman I robbed back home, for her to forgive me ... I felt uplifted when we sang "Amazing Grace" in chapel. It's my favorite song ... My bunkmate kept me awake last night, tossing and turning. I prayed for her ... I thanked Blake for reporting me when I tried to lift the cell phone from Mrs. Walter's purse last month ...

As for myself, I really did thank God that I had a few moments to come up with something and steel my nerves for speaking to a group, which is not the type of thing I relish. The sharp prickle of sweat broke out in my underarms.

When I had to, I said, "I thank God that I could concentrate on sweeping the bunkhouse yesterday. My thoughts did not once go to myself or my problems..."

For one awful moment, I was afraid I had shot myself in the foot. Was that good enough? What if the headmaster demanded details about the problems I might of otherwise been dwelling on? Thanks be to God, he just smiled and nodded, made a gracious move of his hand toward my sweet reward. I went to the table, took the next-to-last unopened candy, and slit the wrapper with my fingernail.

It wasn't particularly difficult to peek at the wavy chocolate, the typical drip pattern on top, then set the candy down again. Even with the smell flooding my nostrils, I knew I wasn't about to humiliate myself by showing any outward sign of struggling with temptation. One girl had hummed a long "Mmmm!" while holding the thing to her face, like she could hardly stand to wait, but then she put it back anyway. Fitzsimmons chuckled and shook a finger. The whole show was such obvious suck-up, no one with a shred of self-respect would go any further.

It all made me feel miserable. So stupid. Like dog-training.

After me, only Annalee had yet to speak.

While most of us took our turns, Mr. Fitzsimmons had hunched forward, half-closing his eyes, a perfect image of close listening. He offered such words as, "Praise the Lord," and "Glorify!" from time to time.

Now he leaned back in his chair, crossed arms over his chest.

He said, "And as for you, Miss Annalee?"

She waited to be called on, but then spoke right up.

"I have forgiven my family, my mother and father, for taking me away from my home and sending me here. I have come to understand why they did that, and how they believed it was the best thing in the world they ever could do for me. To help me and save my immortal soul. What greater love could they have? So I forgive them. Even though it broke my heart, at first. My parents are kind, wonderful human beings. I miss them and all my family, my little brothers, and my cousins. I miss my bedroom and our house and yard and helping my mother cook casserole dinners ..."

Everyone stared. Some of the girls got big eyes, shocked faces. Annalee sounded sincere enough, but she truly could not seem to shut up.

When she finally took a pause, Mr. Fitzsimmons handed her a chance to talk some more.

"That's well and good, Annalee," he stated. "So can we say you have accepted that it is for your salvation that you are here, learning and growing in Christ?"

"Oh, yes. Well and good. So good. I am learning and growing in Christ. I love God and I love my family. I miss my brothers and all my friends and my school and our home church, even Mrs. Mossman in history class..."

Finally, the Headmaster said, "Very well."

He gestured for her to do the candy bit.

Annalee complied.

To round out the chat, each of us had to recite a Bible verse that we had memorized in the past week. Next, we crossed arms over our laps, took hold of hands, and recited the Lord's Prayer. Finally, there came a long pause, during which Mr. Fitzsimmons cast his eyes from one of us to another with fiendish glints and a spreading grin, until at last, he said, "Yes, you may!" granting us permission to take and eat our candies.

Most moved quickly. A few held back for half a moment. There was elbowing and a whispered, *Watch it!* or two.

In seconds flat, those sweet morsels were gone.

Wrappers rustled in a wastebasket that the headmaster carried around the circle.

Girls murmured, *Thank you, sir. Thanks, Mr. Fitzsimmons. Thank you so much.*

Back at the center, he lifted his wide arms and said, "The book of Proverbs tells us: 'Charm is deceitful! Beauty is vain! But a woman who fears the Lord shall be praised.'"

And all God's good girls echoed, "Amen!"

His arms went up a bit higher. The fingers on his right hand beckoned.

Following Molly's example, each of us stepped forward and gave the headmaster a hug. He recited our names without a hitch: "Bless you, Destiny! God loves you, Rachel. Good girl, Tiffany ..."

Some girls got an extra stroke down the back of their heads with his wide palm.

We filed out of the office and down the stairs.

Outside, as we descended the porch, I could hear Annalee whispering to herself, but she didn't speak to me, so I didn't fall in with her. But as Maxwell brought up the rear, Annalee stepped close again and nudged me with her shoulder. She pointed with her chin. I glanced back and saw Maxwell slipping several Mars bars in the pocket of her jacket. It looked like she'd been rewarded with at least three.

* * *

"DID YOUR MOMMA KNOW about this shit that went on?" Bobby asked. "She couldn't of wanted you going through that—beatdowns, head trips. No way."

"I said already, B.F., they censored our mail. You couldn't write about punishments or any bad things that happened. You couldn't even say, 'Please bring me home. I'll do better.' Write that in a letter, it'd just get torn up. You'd have to start all over. They didn't want people leaving the Program early. Monthly fees to consider."

My cousin blew a deep breath and shook his head like my story had dislodged his brain. That sympathy coming my way kept it pouring out of me as if my talking was a ripe seed pod finally ready to burst open.

Truly, I thought of Annalee when I found myself in that place where I couldn't stop talking.

* * *

WITH ALL THE RESTRICTIONS on private conversations, it was hard to believe that some girls actually made friends at The Ministry. That may have been easier on me than on some others, because I've always been more or less fine being lonely. I hum songs or make up stories, and under normal conditions I can go quite a long time without chatting to anybody.

Even so, I felt touched that Annalee had reached out to me. Next time I cleaned the big house, I pocketed a half-dozen of the nice tissues she asked about. At chapel I managed to pass them to her inside of a hymnal. Her face lit up so bright when she saw that, I got a sick feeling every elder in the church house was going to come wail on the both of us with their Very Cruels.

But evidently, no one noticed a thing.

Annalee made a discreet thumbs-up by the side of her knee.

Later that week, she turned up on kitchen duty.

The two of us wound up washing and peeling carrots at the big double-sink under the window that looked out to the vegetable patch where spinach and chard were beginning to brighten in the thin sunshine. It was a pleasant spot, and with our backs to everyone else in the room, we had a perfect chance to talk with water running.

Annalee spoke without looking toward me.

"I've gone to more Big-Daddy chats than anybody here, except some of the elders. I been stuck in here for seven months, three weeks, and four days. I'm just thankful Ol' Fitz let me leave with the rest of you'uns when it was over last time. He usually holds me back for 'special counseling.' Ya see, Miss Ohio, I am a born-this-way queer. Or dyke, if you prefer that term. I like girls the way most girls like boys, ya see. Does that terrify you? I don't push it, or nothin'. To each their own, in my book."

She cast a sidelong look my way.

I said, "Not especially."

I had never met a queer person before, to my knowledge. But it didn't strike me as the worst thing in the world.

"Last year, my parents caught me kissing a 38-year-old female friend of the family. An aunt by marriage, in fact, but now divorced. Guess what. Girl, you'd of thought the world was ending. They are keeping me here until I'm ready to swear I've changed my spots. You've heard of the leopard that can't change spots? That's me: No magic wand, no flippin' way. So I can swear to the impossible, or I can stay here till my eighteenth birthday, whichever comes first. Seeing as I only just turned seventeen in January, I've got a ways to go. So I'm almost ready—like, right *on the verge* of ready—to swear I have gone straight."

She raised a hand to push the blue bandana up her forehead. "It's just not so flippin' easy."

"You don't want to lie?" I asked. "Or you don't want to change?"

She gave a short laugh. "*Can't* change. But *do* want to lie. Just not so easy."

The trustee called us to hurry up and chop those carrots.

"Here's what I like about you, Ohio—" We gathered up the peeled vegetables and headed for the chopping table. "I can tell you're not a fanatic. You've got a human heart. Take good care of it."

Next time we had a chance to talk, Annalee explained her situation in greater detail. We were sitting together in the dining hall for Thursday movie night, when the AV equipment went haywire and someone had to figure out the problem. Spontaneous chatter broke out all over the room, while the technical struggle ensued.

"You know girlfriend Blake over there?" Annalee asked, nodding toward the side wall where several elders had gathered. "You'd never guess what her and me have in common."

I certainly couldn't guess, but the sweet, sideways smile on Annalee's face stirred my curiosity. No one could overhear us amid the numerous conversations. Nonetheless, she leaned close and whispered.

"She's a lesbo. I'm a queer. And we share the same man—our very own Mr. Patrick Fitzsimmons. Yeah, you heard right.

Mr. Fitz performs corrections on girls that get sent here with our type of issues. Remember how I told you I'm almost ready to swear I've reformed? All straightened out and ready to marry a man—Halleluiah! Ya see, swearing's the easy part. Then comes proving: He's going to make me kiss him and let him touch me. It could even go all the way—spread legs, insert the ol' yoo-know-what. All that, so he can vouch for me. 'Yep, she's good to go.' He did it to Blake last year. Had sex with her half a dozen times. To verify she's thoroughly cured of gayness."

My mouth wouldn't even close on hearing this. Finally I said, "That's wacko. That's got to be gossip."

Not that I had some high opinion where Fitzsimmons was concerned. Even so, it was sickening to think he would go to such lengths. The candy game in his office was bad enough.

"You think I'd make this up? Fitz told me hisself."

"What about Mrs. Fitz?"

"He says, 'I'll take the sin of adultery on my soul to save you from the sin of abomination.' Besides, she's fine with whatever keeps us throttled."

I looked across the seats at Blake, the elder who'd administered my first (and so far only) whacks with the Very Cruel. Annalee's story seemed to fit with the unvarying, stern expression Blake kept on her face at all times. Talk about self-control. I'd never seen her smile, not even when she chatted with other elders, some of who were happy to yuck it up in their private moments. Also, it occurred to me that she did avoid bathroom inspections, especially when showers were going on. I'd seen her bring an elder from a different bunkhouse to go in and quiet girls down who were laughing in the shower.

It was disgusting to think Annalee's tale might be true.

"You need to know how bad it can get," Annalee said by way of excuse for upsetting me. "You're not a pure Goody Two-Shoes, I can tell that. But you seem to respect what goes on here. I guess some girls do. Just don't forget there's another side to things."

"What are you going to do? Will you swear?"

"Yeah. I've almost decided. He can do his worst to me—I've gotta get my sweet ass out of here some way."

Right about then, Mrs. Fitzsimmons herself came to the front of the hall with a saucepan and serving spoon, which she proceeded to clang together until everyone fell silent. She announced that Friday night refreshments would be canceled due to our undisciplined behavior this evening.

Chattering like magpies! Laughing like hyenas! Now it was time to line up by bunkhouse for forty minutes on our knees before an early bedtime.

We never did see the ending of that movie.

* * *

IT'S PROBABLY NOT SURPRISING that men were a rarity and items of considerable interest when they did appear at The Ministry. It was said that so many girls had offered themselves to a certain former math teacher that in recent years all male teachers—as well as repairmen, delivery drivers, etcetera—were required to be at least sixty years old.

Annalee's comment: "Age ain't no obstacle for Mr. Fitz."

She had been summoned to his office a couple of times since we last talked. She had taken the pledge, promising never to think of females in sinful ways again, and accepted his kisses on her lips as token of her sincerity.

"I can take it," she told me, but she beat the heels of her hands against her forehead. "I closed my eyes and thought of Natalie Portman. Her black hair, beautiful eyes—but he smells like such a hound! It knocked the fantasy right out of my head. He wants me back at his office another time to make sure. It's revolting. But I can do it. I know I can."

Annalee gave me the Mars bar Mr. Fitz had forked over as her "positive reinforcement." I dropped the wrapper in the bottom of the trash barrel ahead of the potato peelings, next kitchen duty.

* * *

NOW THAT SPRING WAS BRINGING warmer weather, everyone seemed a tiny bit happier, a bit easier. Everyone except me and Annalee, each for our different reasons. I was definitely feeling pregnant by now, my belly a cantaloupe on its way to becoming a watermelon. Every step I took felt like it required two-three times the normal effort.

Mrs. Virland kept saying stuff like, "The Lord gives you strength, girls. The baby gives you energy." But I only wanted to sit in one place and do nothing.

Even for me, though, the atmosphere around the compound seemed a bit brighter. With the sun showing up, it was easier to linger outdoors and find chances to talk on the way between dorms, chapel, classes, meals. Girls were getting caught in fewer infractions, even while risky behavior happened more often.

In spite of my unending desire for rest, it was nice to work outside. The wind didn't bother me. So I did my best to get garden duty. Only a few of us were trusted to weed the vegetable patch. Seems the city girls could not tell a weed from a carrot top to save their souls, so to speak. I got put in charge of that assignment.

That's where I was, scratching at the dirt with a hoe one cool but beautiful afternoon, not a cloud in the sky, when an amazing event took place.

Remember Mrs. Fitzsimmons' Labrador puppies? She never did take me to pet them, but I'd seen a few special girls leash-breaking them here and there on the grounds. In mid-March, Mrs. Fitzsimmons evidently ran an ad in some newspaper, and people started coming out to choose their new dog. Purebred—big bucks! So the rumor mill said.

A nice blue Buick got buzzed in the rolling gate by Mrs. Anders. She waved the driver to park in front of the big house, and a cute young couple in matching khaki and corduroy coats got out, probably in their mid-thirties. Bounding after them, came two elementary-aged boys in plaid shirts and jean-jackets.

Mrs. Fitzsimmons shortly descended from the house and led these folks to a side shed where the half-grown litter spent most of their time. The parents and boys crowded up to the dutch-style door, of which the top half was open. The dad lifted his smaller boy to look over and view the puppies. The older boy stood on tip-toes with Mom's hands on his shoulders.

That shed was built of shaped block, the kind that looks like stone. Overall, it was a compact, square building—I think it may of been an old-time icehouse or some such. It happened that a crew of girls was engaged in whitewashing the outside of it at that very time. There were five or six girls in headscarves, two ladders, several buckets, long-handled implements, and so on. From what I could gather at the distance of the vegetable patch, Mrs. Fitzsimmons directed these girls to go take a breather on her porch, getting them out of the way of the dog-watching activity.

The girls were no doubt happy to take a break. The front porch of the big house was a fine, inviting spot. We never got to sit there, so this was a special privilege of sorts. Girls leaned their tools against the unpainted portion of the shed or laid them on a ground cloth and trooped up the porch steps, arranging themselves on Mrs. Fitzsimmons's elegant wicker furniture, which had lately been brought out of storage somewhere. I observed several smiles among them.

But one girl didn't go along. I could see her against the shed wall on the far side of the house. It was Sarah. I had gotten to know her a little—a constant complainer with pretty tendrils of near-black hair that others loved to braid for her. I wondered what she was doing on a paint crew. As one of us preg-girls, at least seven months along, she was not meant to be dealing with household chemicals, but it looked as though she'd been wielding a small push broom, so maybe her task was knocking down wasp nests or what not. However that may be, when her crew headed up to the porch, she dropped the broom and disappeared in back of the shed. A second later, she peered around the corner, then made a streak—fast as any girl could with that belly—for the Buick parked on the circle drive.

She ran right behind Mrs. Fitzsimmons's back. Half the girls on the porch must've seen her dash around the trunk-end of the car.

From my vantage it seemed clear that a few girls raised their heads and alerted, but not one called an alarm. Sarah came to a crouch by the rear tire on the far side of the car from the shed.

Mrs. Anders was carrying a pair of blond Lab puppies out onto the gravel. She set them down, and they gamboled about, fighting and biting, like the joyous young creatures they were. Mrs. Fitzsimmons was evidently advising the visiting family on some fine points of comparison between the two.

Sarah reached up and grasped the handle of the Buick's rear passenger door. She raised up to look through the windows. She would've been in full view of anyone coming from the dining hall. Or watching out its windows.

But there she bided her time.

Those lucky little boys soon chose their puppy. They laughed as it licked their faces and nibbled at their sleeves. The mom pulled out a checkbook. Mrs. Fitzsimmons was all smiles. I could hear the alto notes of her voice telling that family to "Come back and see us."

Sarah had learned some smarts since wintertime when she tried to blackmail Mrs. Virland and got beat for her trouble. She watched until the boys brought their new baby Lab right up to the car door. At the exact moment the elder boy pulled the handle on the other side, she did the same on hers. She was in the Buick, hunkered between the seats, before those kids pulled their door open.

The tall one released the puppy onto the backseat. As he climbed in after, the unexpected visitor's presence registered on his face. The little brother ran to the far side, where the door was already ajar, and climbed in there. Both boys stared at the hunched figure between them. I couldn't see, but clearly imagined the intensity of Sarah's big brown eyes as she spared no effort to convince them to keep silent.

Help her play hide'n'seek.

Another stroke of luck: Mrs. Fitzsimmons stopped well short of the visitors' car, stood smiling for a moment, gave a wave, then headed back to her porch.

The girls sitting up there now faced a real dilemma.

The parents, meanwhile, came up to their car, perceived their boys engaged in some strange conversation, and stood for a moment leaning in their respective doors, eyes trained on a young woman in the back who now turned every power she could muster to them.

Please, take me to town! Just give me a ride. I need to call my family. I'm not supposed to be here. They beat me here, they'll beat me again if you don't take me...

I imagined Sarah's pleas, laying it on thick. Maybe she still had some bruises to display—undeniable proof of mistreatment. In the chilly March breeze, I closed my eyes and leaned on my hoe, dreading what would come next. I could hear the whoosh of crows wings overhead and their harsh *Caw-aw!* as they went about the business of policing the onset of spring.

When I looked again, the man and woman had gotten into the front seats of their car. They pulled the doors shut.

I saw Sarah's head appear between the two boys. She sat in the middle of the backseat. The father started the car. He pulled around, onto the main drive. The Buick was rolling toward the gate. I could see that the mother was turned, looking at Sarah. I imagined dismay written all over her face.

But Mrs. Fitzsimmons had clearly got wind.

She was headed back down the steps, calling to Mrs. Anders at the switchbox by the gate. A girl was dispatched from the porch to fetch Mr. Fitz from up in the house. He soon appeared, squinting his eyes and buttoning his suit coat. With a look that I took for forced unconcern, he descended to the driveway at a stately pace.

All while the man in the car blew his horn and attempted to negotiate with Anders.

My sweet Jesus, I said to myself. They are helping her. They are springing her out of here.

Hoe still in my hand, I couldn't stop myself from walking toward the house and the gate. On all sides, people seemed to share my fascination. Those girls poured off the porch, and a dozen or more came out of the dining hall, including elders and trustees. I joined the crowd that shaped up in a horseshoe about a dozen feet back from the car.

Everyone was whispering. They all seemed to know what had happened, but no one knew what to expect.

Mr. and Mrs. Fitzsimmons broke through our ranks, smiles pasted on their faces. He went to the driver's side window, she to the shotgun seat, and they launched into damage control.

I could hear most of what was said.

"Sarah, what's come over you? We thought you had settled in so nicely ..."

"You're looking at a serious liability, young man. Abetting a runaway, a pregnant minor, at that ..."

"Her family sent her to us. It is their wish for their daughter to be here ..."

"No, we don't use any sort of corporal punishment. I assure you ..."

"The girls are happy here. I don't know what's got into our Sarah ..."

That sweet family tried to hold their own. It sounded like the mother and the little boy were crying.

Sarah screamed and begged. It was terrible.

The Fitzes kept up their threats and implications, but without ever raising voices or appearing riled. Suddenly, all went quiet. They looked to be discussing inside the car.

Mrs. Fitz stepped away and came toward us gawkers. "Everyone—let's have a song. Soothe the waters. Let's sing 'The Balm of Gilead.'"

I think it was Mrs. Lemoyne who obliged by striking up the melody. Some girls sang along. Not me, not everyone. Several were agog and couldn't sing even if they wanted to. But the tune rose up.

After a long, long moment, the father emerged from the car. He reached to open the backdoor, and the elder of the two boys slid out. He stood like a little sentinel beside his father, a frown on his face. Mr. Fitzsimmons reached a hand into the car, like some butler on Downton Abbey, and helped Sarah emerge. She kept her eyes on the ground. Speaking in his soft, fatherly voice, Mr. Fitz placed an arm around her shoulders and walked her toward the big house as if all she needed was half an hour on the fainting couch.

When she was well away, inside, the gate rolled open.

The Buick departed slowly, like a blue hearse.

The song broke off unevenly.

Mrs. Fitz ordered everyone present to the chapel to await further deployment. Over the rest of the afternoon, everyone was questioned on what we saw and what we thought it all meant.

Caught in the dragnet, I could not escape suspicion of having witnessed Sarah's attempt without notifying authorities. Along with most of the paint crew, I had to stand in a cold shower for ten minutes under threat of Very Cruels. If I hadn't been pregnant, I would of missed dinner as well. We all got extra work duty, but mine was back in the vegetable patch so that was no great hardship.

We all thought Sarah would be beaten, locked in a closet for days, too cramped to lie down, and forced to crawl around the compound until her hands and knees bled. In fact, they kept her at the big house. Warm and toasty. Nobody saw what happened there, and we got no chance to talk to her. But exactly four days later, a small white Toyota arrived at the gate, and Mrs. Fitz was observed walking Sarah out to meet it. The driver, a woman, emerged onto the greening lawn, and the three of them stood in a huddle for several minutes, after which the unknown woman opened the passenger door, and Sarah got in with a small canvas bag.

The Toyota sailed out the gate, and Sarah was not seen again. Some said the woman from the Buick must have called her parents. Her family was taking her back.

Others argued, No way. That Toyota lady was no relation. Family would of hugged her after all this time, no matter how sinful she'd been.

No, they were sending her to a Catholic home in St. Louis till after the baby.

Maybe so, but her family had agreed to let her keep the baby—she could work in their business and care for the kid in the backroom during the day.

No, they meant to pass the baby off as her sister—Mom's change-of-life child.

Well, maybe, but they were suing The Ministry, for sure.

No, Mr. Fitz had bought them off. Like he also bought off the puppy-buying family who claimed their boys had been traumatized by Sarah's dramatics.

No one had a clue.

All we could know for certain was that there appeared to be no leaks. No reporters came nosing around. Nothing of the kind.

And the remaining puppies were taken to the Lemoyne farm and sold off from there.

* * *

"WHOA, NELLY. HOLD UP," Bobby says. "What about *your* baby? You said your dear momma offered to have her raised by Jo Beth. As your niece. That ain't what happened."

"Well, duh."

I rise to my feet and stretch. The stone pedestal under my butt has got to feeling hard and cold. In fact, the evening is cooling off quick now with gusts of wind riffling the tops of the cemetery pines. Clouds in the west are rust-colored under a layer of deep-dark blue. Late rays of sun escape through their cracks. But off to the southeast, a thunderhead is boiling up. Where it catches the sun, the color is pink rising to stark white. Behind that, a mass of smoky gray.

I see a family of hawks riding the forward air of those clouds like people posted on rising steps of a vast staircase. Without a single wing-flap, they float onward like ghosts that don't move their feet. I count three, four, five hawks.

A flash of lightning brightens a cavern in the cloud for an instant. It crosses my mind to wonder: If one bird fell from the sky, would God really know or care? I lift my hair to let the breeze cool my neck.

"You want to get going?" I ask. "Ain't you bored of this old story?"

Bobby says, "Naw. You keep on."

He pats the stone, so I sit back beside him.

"Crack me one of those, whatever's left in the bag," he says, chin toward our assortment.

There's a mini Jack Daniels. I pass it over. Bobby paws a pill from his collection, washes it down. Looked like a benny.

At that point, no, I did not bother objecting to his substance abuse. Why should I? It was clear he would do as he pleased. And I'll admit, I'd got wrapped up in my own talking by then. My head was off in a new place, revisiting the old times as a different person than I'd been back when.

"So you didn't want that—" Bobby says, "—your baby growing up under your nose but belonging to somebody else. So near and yet so far, like they say."

He drops the bottle back in the bag, where it makes a soft *clink* on the other empties. With a slight grunt and shove, he gets to his feet, swipes at a low branch and rips off a juicy twig. It fills the air with a pitchy pine smell that gets stronger as he proceeds to strip off the long needles and scatter them down while he walks in a circle.

Makes me think of an angry farm woman feeding chickens.

"So let me get it straight—my sweet cuz Jo Beth woulda been in charge of all the kid-rearin' decisions, the day-by-day doings. If she saw fit to slap your child or whup her with the ruler for sucking her thumb—why, you'd just have to onlook and suck it up. Or maybe say something that she'd grouse about and ignore. Is that it?"

I shrug, but Bobby doesn't appear to need an answer.

"And whatsisname, Jay, the Parkersburg rock star, would be raising this child that's no kin to him alongside his own kid with never any show of favorites nor unfairness." He brakes the pine twig and tosses two pieces in opposite directions. "Yeah. I can well figure, that might not sound good to you, LaDene."

Of course, he'd understood right. While I was sweeping floors out in Missouri, I came to an understanding with myself. I did not want that.

Every Sunday afternoon, I would receive my little stash of mail from home. All pre-opened with a slit across the top. Sometimes it was just the regular letter from Momma, sometimes with a card or two from my sisters or aunts. My father never wrote. That wasn't his way, but Momma always mentioned him, said he loved and missed me, forgave me for everything, and wanted me home soon. So soon.

I was required to write one letter to my parents, minimum, every week. If I couldn't get this accomplished on Sunday, then I could use part of Bible Study class during the week. Either way, it had to get written or I would face closet-time. Like clockwork, I fulfilled this duty, handing my letters to the trustee for "proof-reading" and mailing. Many times I saw letters returned to girls who'd foolishly written "negative sentiments" that they were expected to omit, starting over from "Dear Mom and Dad," by longhand.

I had no trouble doing my own censorship. The trustees would always tell me, "Very nice job," and accept my first drafts. But for weeks on end, I never wrote back about The Plan.

My standard effort went about like this—

Dear Momma and Daddy, Effie and Jo Beth,

It is turning nice and warm here. Our walks every morning and evening are nice. We get a good deal of sun. The fields around The Ministry Campus are greening up and trees are budded out. Yesterday one of those big herons flew over like the ones that live on the river at home. I don't know where they fish around here, but they do live here.

I miss home and miss all of you and wish you could come visit me here. I bet you would like Missouri. It is called the "show-me state," like the Doubting Thomas. But I know you all have to work and can't get away for a long trip.

We sing many songs here that I know from our King's Way Church, like "Blessed Be the Tie That Binds" and "Lights of Home." I have memorized dozens of Psalms and other verses. My favorite is from Psalm 34, "The Lord is close to all whose hearts are crushed by pain, and he is always ready to restore the repentant one."

I have learned to make macaroni and cheese and to bake cornbread and biscuits from scratch. Later we may learn to make jam. So I will be a bigger help when I come home.

I also learned to fix holes in the toes of socks by darning. This saves on buying lots of new socks. You use a thing shaped like an egg called a darner. It is fun to do.

Love to all,
LaDene Faye Howell

MANY OF MOMMA'S LETTERS referred to the plan for the baby. It was not hard to tell she wanted me to come out and flat say it—that I was on board: Swear I would keep the secret forever. She wrote things like, "You must understand that it can never be mentioned. Your sister must always be considered as the 'Real Mother.' I know you can do it. What do you think?"

Week after week, I didn't comment on that. But I was thinking about it.

* * *

A different thing that happened shortly after Sarah's escape sobered up everyone's springtime mood. It actually took
place on a rainy Wednesday afternoon, as if to emphasize
that we'd all let the sunshine go to our heads and needed to
remember the cold reality and cruel wages of sin.

At chapel that day, Mr. Fitz led the usual prayers and
readings. He called on the Lord to protect His vulnerable
lambs from the outrages of this fallen world. Naturally, we all
took note that a large, middle-aged man in some type of police uniform was seated in a side pew by the west door, quietly
holding a cowboy hat on his lap as he bided his time.

After opening prayers, Mr. Fitz announced that our
special guest was Butler County Sheriff's Deputy Somebody-
or-Other, who had, "Come to our midst to share a message
about purity and sanctity and how we must do all we can to
preserve them."

Leaving his hat on the pew, the man rose and crossed
the floor. After a somber handshake with our headmaster, he
smoothed the already slicked-back strands of dark hair on
his skull. He leaned into the pulpit and spoke in a voice that
managed to alternate from low to harsh in attention-grab-
bing succession.

"Thanks for the invitation to be here today, Reverend. I'm
always happy to address young people. I do have an important
message for all the ladies here in your ministry. It's a message
that tends to get forgot just a little too easy. In the law enforcement profession, we encounter reminders pretty near every day
that our society has let morals and respect fall by the wayside
in preference for self-indulgent pleasures and gratification.

"Now, anybody can see the loss of morals in movies and
entertainment nowadays. The R-rated scenes and worse.

Video games. The glorification of debauchery. You also see it in real events—on the news, in broken families, broken schools, parents struggling to teach our children good values when Hollywood teaches the opposite..."

I imagined how Annalee might say, *I'm afraid not just anybody can see that, Sir. We're not allowed to watch movies in here, nor even the news on TV.*

I guess it was a sign of how close we'd gotten that her type of commentary came into my head without her directly saying it. I could even hear the sweet voice she would use to tell the sheriff something like this.

But the man was barely getting warm to his topic.

"Well, let me tell you—in law enforcement, we see up-close and firsthand exactly what comes from that loss of morals. We see the assaults, the injuries, and yes, even loss of innocent life. It is no laughing matter..."

I'm quite sure no one had laughed, nor even smiled, but here the sheriff took a pause, lowered his head, and swept his gaze over us, from one side of church to the other. Like he could banish wrong-thinking by sheer force of eye-power.

"Only last month we found a young woman, no older than some of you here, dead in her car with a broken neck, smashed on a tree on the side of County Road 9. Come to find out, she would've been a mother in another half year or so. Her family didn't even know that. Maybe she didn't even know. But instead of bringing her child into this world, giving her family a grandchild and building a life, she got drunk, got behind the wheel, and snuffed out two young souls for the price of one.

"Why is it, girls today think they should be able to do whatever the boys do? Don't y'all want to be on the smart side of the equation? No way! These days it's all, 'Girls just wanna have fun!' Girls just wanna be free, wanna run with the wolves! Girls think they should be able to go wherever they want, wherever boys go, broad daylight, after dark, no limits! They go off with girlfriends, with boyfriends, with strange men they met on the internet—men who tell the most outrageous lies. And girls believe them. They think fair is fair. Equal rights for all.

"But let me tell you. Girls get drunk, girls go wherever, go off on their own—they do *not* get treated fair or equal. Girls get treated *way worse*—"

He banged the wooden pulpit with his large fist.

Now that it was clear what we were in for, the hall, which had been quiet before, fell silent like everybody had stopped breathing. The sheriff took that harnessed attention and proceeded to inform us about every rape and murder he had attended (or maybe just heard tell of) over most of his law enforcement career.

He detailed the ones where, "She didn't just get it the way God intended. She got it every way physically possible."

He dwelt on the ones where, "Pain was the last thing she experienced in her short life."

He asked, how young was the youngest among us?

When Mr. Fitz answered that we presently had a few thirteen-year olds in residence, he said, "I've seen a girl aged 12 all torn up from what men are ready to do when y'all get careless, when you go off by yourselves, when you get drunk or use drugs."

The silence didn't last. Girls on both sides of me had started crying. The lucky ones with tissues in their pockets blew their noses.

Nobody said a word. Nobody whispered.

Eventually, the sheriff moved on to talking about heartsick parents. The father of the murdered girl. The mother of the raped twelve-year old. The grandparents who blamed themselves. Parents who drowned their unbearable sorrow, lost jobs, committed suicide. The little brothers and sisters left behind when grief claimed its bonus victims.

Kindly Mrs. Virland took pity and started down the aisle with a tissue box, passing handfuls to the pews. I couldn't even tell when our guest speaker finally wrapped it up. I got too busy handing tissues around.

It was a genuine relief to see Mr. Fitzsimmons return to the pulpit. He pumped the sheriff's hand again, clapped his shoulder. He said, "Thank you, deputy," in a grave tone. Looking to us, he added, "Girls—let's show our appreciation."

He led a subdued round of applause, followed by a lengthy prayer. Lots of contrition, lots of entreaties to keep our minds pure and protected.

At long last, we were dismissed. We had to file past the sheriff—deputy, I guess—who stood by the exit door, smiling and nodding at us. He patted some of the weepers on the head, actually gave hugs to those who thanked him for sharing his message.

I refused to look at him. Kept my head down as if I was still praying. Right then, I actually didn't care if every word he'd said was true (which I kind of doubted. Had he really been there for everything, seen all that firsthand? How did he know all the details—what someone thought or prayed with her final breath?). He had no right to dump such ugly stories on a captured audience. I would of liked to be the pregnant girl who lost her lunch in the middle of his speech, in the middle of chapel. And got to leave early. Too bad you can't turn it off and on.

The strange thing was, devastated as everybody felt right then, I know I heard more sharp bursts of laughter in the days after the speech than ever before. Not that first night— at first, people did seem extra quiet. But it wore off fast.

And over the next week, there were fatherly chats at the big house every day. Enough that everyone got to attend, regardless of recent infractions. On Friday, there were two in one day.

* * *

THERE WAS ONE MAN—much younger than Mr. Fitzsimmons, around forty years of age—who was trusted to step foot on The Ministry campus without succumbing to seduction or smuggling anybody out. That was Mr. Fitz's incorruptible nephew, our musical director. Mr. Dyson's main job was directing a group of twelve girls who lived together in the smallest—allegedly the nicest—bunkhouse. The group was called The Sweet Rebekahs. They practiced continually and sang for us at church service most Sundays.

These girls never got punishments, weren't subjected to close supervision by elders, and took actual classes on computers that counted toward high school graduation. They could even earn college credit. The girls were selected to be in the group for their exemplary behavior and musical skills.

Naturally, we were not allowed to talk to them.

"They should put you in that group," Annalee said. It was a semi-sunny April day when I had finagled for us to do garden duty together. "You sing like a veri-table angel."

"There's no pregnant girls in that group," I said.

"They should take you anyways. Course, you'd have to be willing to talk about the sins you committed. That's what those girls do. Come summer, they travel around with Mrs. or Mr. Fitz to all different churches. They sing and testify on how they got reformed here. Praise be to the Four Pillars. They rake in donations. It's a racket."

"I couldn't do that," I said.

"I know." She gave a short laugh. "Still. You should be in that group. You can sing for real."

It was a joke between us that we were friends because she

loved to talk and I hated it. That's not strictly true, as you can
tell, but in those days, I was definitely quiet. Giving a testimo-
ny would be like the end of the world to me.

I leaned on my hoe, looked down at Annalee clipping
spinach for the kitchen. That frizzy hair of hers, towhead like
a child, had grown out to where she now wore a small ponytail that curled on her neck like a bun.

"So how much longer are you stuck here?" I asked. "You
swore to Mr. Fitz about goin' straight, right? He's s'posed to
send you home."

I knew she had been avoiding this topic while she gabbed
about any and everything else she could think of.

"Not so easy. Not easy, at all. No no no—"

She seemed to be talking to the ground, hacking green
leaves furiously.

"What's the problem? He wants more proof of
heterosex-stuff?"

She didn't answer. Sniffed real loud through her nose. All at
once, she started gasping like a panic attack, stopped clipping
the spinach and, instead, gripped the kitchen shears by both
handles and hammered the point end into her other palm.

She made an awful whimpery sound.

"Don't be doing that! What's wrong with you?"

I knelt down and yanked the shears away. Her hand
wasn't dripping blood, but it glowed red and spotty.

She let her head hang like her neck was broke and heaved
a ragged breath. "He makes me consent to everything. Makes
me say, 'Yes, I want that,' like some little bitch. And it has to
convince him. It's so disgusting. I want to die—"

I glanced around and took a chance, put a hand on her
shoulder. "Did he touch you? More than kissing?"

She usually enjoyed getting all cocky, claiming she could
stand whatever Fitz dished out. But not now. "Just my chest.

My tits." She sucked air like the very thought knocked the wind out of her.

"And he's gonna do more?"

"I couldn't convince him! Must of flinched or gagged. I don't know what I did. I couldn't pull it off—"

"Holy Mother—" I had taken to praying in some strange ways by that time.

Annalee shrugged my hand off. "Cut it out. They can see from the kitchen." She rocked her weight and got to her feet, gave me a hand to stand up.

My eight-month gut weighed me down.

Not looking me in the face, Annalee wiped her hands furiously on her thighs and said in a breathless voice, "You can get to the tools, right? In the garage? LaDene, you gotta help me."

With a jerk of her chin, she started toward the three-car garage, a pre-fab metal structure that stood a bit off by itself behind the big house. Trustees' cars were parked along one side and in back. On the wall toward the garden, an entry door opened to a stall-like room where we stored tools. I had been entrusted with the combination for the lock on this door.

We left the steel bowl of spinach where it sat on the ground. I dropped the scissors into the bowl, left the hoe prone on the ground.

"What the fuck, Annalee. What am I helping you with?"

This was clearly dire times. I spun the combination lock and got the door open. We stepped into the storage area.

"You gotta help me," she said again, her voice shaking. "I know how it's done. I just can't do it myself—"

Breathing like we'd run five miles, she lifted down the heavy spade. Handed it to me. She turned her left foot to one side and leaned with her arm onto a shelf of empty plant pots, her leg aslant.

"Use the blunt edge. The side. Hard as you can."

I figured out she wanted me to break her ankle. "Jesus Christ, Annalee—"

"You have to. It's the only way. A real injury—they'll send me to a hospital. Otherwise, he's gonna make me say I want it. He'll fuck me and he still won't let me go home 'cause I can't convince him."

Her breath came in dry little sobs, but real tears rolled down her cheeks. Red ovals glowed there like coals.

My arms went weak, but I managed to lift the shovel shoulder-high. Looked at her size-five foot in tennies and white socks. It seemed impossible, but I took a firm breath. I dropped the shovel's bent edge onto her ankle.

She stifled a yell, sobbed harder. "Again. It didn't crack."

I lifted, breathed, slammed down harder. Truly, I wanted to help. But the picture of a bone popping out sprang into my mind. It brought up the nausea. After three tries, we were both at wits' end.

"It'll bruise something fierce," I said. "Just limp and tell 'em you can't walk. Say it's broken."

"Convincing," she whispered. "Has to be real."

I was at a loss.

"Help. Help me get up here—" Gulping for air, she pushed aside the flowerpots. One fell and smashed on the concrete floor.

I upended a bucket, steadied her by the arm while she clambered onto the shelf, about five feet above the floor. Still a chunky girl, though less than she was months ago, she only fit partway, gripping and balancing.

"I'll do it," she said. "Just, don't let me skid. It won't break if I do."

A snow shovel stood propped in the corner—a good-sized target. I put the spade back on the wall and grabbed this one, set the backside toward her.

"Aim your foot at this," I said.

I braced myself against the opposite wall, the shovel handle pressed to my shoulder.

Annalee kept her foot bent up. She whispered hot quick words. Shoved off.

The crack was muffled but sickening. Annalee screamed. Went down on her ass. Waved her hands something wild, rolled side to side.

I thought I would faint. Bent over and lost my lunch—*splat*. Gripped the shovel handle to keep from sinking down.

A breeze creaked the half-open door. It carried voices—girls coming from the flowerbed, fetching rakes, trowels, whatever? Still half bent-over, I peeked out, peered around.

No one was nearby, thank the Lord.

Annalee rolled up on all fours, moaned like an animal. I could hear her deep breaths, slower now. A sound rose from her throat that sounded like crazed joy. From the nursing knowledge I now possess, I am sure she was getting a burst of analgesic endorphins. At the time, though, it looked like she was dying. Her face had gone a whitish green, beaded all over with sweat.

But her voice quaked with ecstasy. "You, girl—you are my savior."

It smelled like she had shat herself. Or was it me? No, must be her.

She crawled to the door. "Come on," she whispered. "Lock up."

Shaky, realizing the peril of our situation, I did the job quick. Replaced the combination lock while Annalee crawled out on the grass.

Wispy white clouds had dimmed the sun. No one was around. Only a Phys. Ed. group starting their afternoon run way up by the entry gate across the compound from us. I could see that Blake was supervising, bringing up the rear at a fast walk.

I tried to help Annalee to her feet. "Lean on me."

"Nah. You weren't here. Get inside." She insisted. "Take the greens. Say you left me out here to—What can you say I was doing?"

"Stake the tomatoes. We were gonna stake tomatoes."

"I tripped on somethin'—"

"Trip on a cinder block."

A row of blocks edged one side of the vegetable patch, for squashes to grow on, or some such.

"Right," she breathed. "So go."

I left her, on her side, wedging her toe into the square of a cinder block.

Blake found Annalee. She directed the Phys. Ed. girls to carry her into the dining hall, two on each limb. The evening cook, Mrs. Davids, cut off Annalee's shoe and sock with the same shears we'd used in the garden. She packed the purple lump of a foot in ice, wrapped in a towel.

Nobody commented on the dribbles of shit that trailed on the dining hall floor.

Perhaps because I spoke so seldom, nobody appeared to suspect that I might dissemble. I grabbed a handful of rags and ran to my work partner, crying, "What on earth happened?"

No one objected that I sit with Annalee while the Fitzsimmonses were notified. I got her cleaned up a little. "Don't let him come," she whispered. "Please, Jesus, not him. He'll look at me. He'll know, it was me. Please, Jesus."

"You are delirious," I said for all to hear. "Try and relax. Help is coming."

The headmistress arrived in a flurry, in her sky-blue pant suit. She knelt by Annalee's chair and viewed the injury. The ankle was double normal size. Annalee slumped, squeezed her eyes shut.

Mrs. Fitzsimmons asked a few questions.

I let Blake answer: Heard a scream, saw Blanchard on the ground, tomato stakes, cinder block.

The day shift was ending right about then, and trustees preparing to drive home. Mrs. Lemoyne ventured into the dining hall. Word had spread fast. She offered to drive to the emergency room in Butler. Not much out of her way.

Mrs. Fitzsimmons would notify the parents and follow along after.

The Phys. Ed. girls were told to stop gabbing and get back to their run. Blake herded them outside. Mrs. Davids found a pair of crutches in a closet. She and I managed to get Annalee out to Mrs. Lemoyne's truck.

I didn't know if she could keep anything down, but I passed Annalee a fresh bread roll from the kitchen before the door was slammed and she rode away. I knew she put great store in small comforts. She made a small wave from the window of the truck and tipped her head to one side, looking at me. No one prevented me from standing there until they drove out the gate and out of sight down the road.

Now I had no friend at all. But the hand of Fate reached out, and a few days later, I had cause to remember Annalee saying I sang like an angel.

Mr. Dyson included me in a choir of fifteen girls he selected to learn a special set of songs (a "cantata") for Easter service. Thereafter, six of us were invited to become understudies for the traveling ensemble that Annalee had talked about. Soon, I was excused from afternoon work to attend music practice. I moved my things to the special bunkhouse. The beds were more comfy, the sheets nicer than in the larger dorm, and the windows had flowered curtains instead of plain blinds.

After a week or two, I even got to use a computer—an antique variety, but still—and I signed up for two courses on-line.

I was a Sweet Rebekah.

* * *

BOBBY HAS LONG SINCE FINISHED his last cigarette. By the way he's rubbing his arms and belly, I can tell he's ready for the next one.

But he asks, "So that's why you stayed gone so long? I remember, it was some kinda scandal. Momma put a nice face on it—you had a little chance to perform for people, travel around some. Still. I know your folks took it hard."

All my talking is still a thrill, but I'm starting to feel a little down from the sad parts. It was exciting to think I had a story to tell that could engross Bobby so much. But digging into the bad times has my mind straying to the bag of bottles at our feet. Mostly empties, but there's a mini-Smirnoff left. I twist it open. More palatable with pomegranate, but hey—I'm ready to settle for what's available.

"We need supplies," Bobby says. "This truth-telling is dry work. What say we hit the IGA? Then I'll show you a little surprise. My country estate, so to say."

It is dusk now. The wind has picked up considerably, and even the oak trees are rustling. A big rhododendron bush bends over the path before us. As we start down the Indian mound, I put out my hand for the car keys, but Bobby just gives them a jingle in his fist. Jokes about stealing my car.

He says I'm a good sport to let him drive—gives him a "sense of agency" after being locked up for four years. He laughs about that.

We get into the car and take off. Bobby turns up Muskingum Drive, north to the outskirts.

Here's where shit starts going down.

Part III

Like I told you, we were approaching the Speedway on the east side of Highway 60 when Bobby kind of hunches forward in the driver's seat and cranes his neck, staring hard at the store, back past the gas pumps. Out of nowhere he asks me, "Who's that old coot coming out the door there?"

He slows way down while I take a look. I see a pulled-together type older gentleman. Tall and lean. He's in dark-blue jeans and a short-sleeve, checked button shirt. Clean shaven, salt'n'pepper hair in a trim burr.

I say, "Kinda looks like old Mr. Rutherford." Or words to that effect.

The main thing I recognized was the nose-in-the-air type of look he always had when he ventured into the hallways among us lowly students. Like he could oversee the crowds of us from on high but never really recognize anyone or even look an individual in the face. And the same now, like he's not really a small-town hick like everybody else around, even when he's just toting a two-liter bottle of pop and chips home on a Friday night.

We'd talked about going to the IGA, but instead Bobby makes a quick turn and parks in front of the Speedway, where the old man has stopped mid-stride to take a look at the newspaper box.

Bobby whips out a pair of twenty-dollar bills from somewhere. Tells me to pick up drinks and smokes. "Camel filters and whatever you want, Darlin'."

Fine with me. I take the money and go to the door.

No, not one thing was said between us to indicate a "criminal intent," nor plan of any sort. Still just out cruising.

As I passed him, it looked like maybe Mr. Rutherford was putting away his change, maybe reading the headlines. He had a plastic bag in each hand, or maybe one on his arm.

Why would I speak to him? I wasn't certain it was my old principal, and even on the off-chance it was him, I don't expect people to remember LaDene Howell from a few weeks of school twelve years ago.

I go inside. Grab an eight-pack of Little Kings—somehow I thought that'd be good for a laugh. Also a couple Arizona ice teas, a bag of white cheddar popcorn, handful of jerky. At the checkout, I ask for the cigs and three mini-bottles each of Crown and Smirnoff.

I'm thinking that'll slow down the drinking better than if I bought a fifth. A rationing program, so to say. Ha-ha.

Did I think a bedroom might be in our mutual future? Yeah, it crossed my mind. I knew I could use a hug after all those bad memories we revisited. There goes my pipe dream again.

Back outside, a different surprise awaited.

Bobby has a map spread out on the hood of my car. Must of come from my glove box. He's got the old man on the passenger's side with him, leaned over, looking at this map. Bobby's voice sounds more West Virginia than usual, saying something like, "I don't git up yere t'Ohio real of-ten so I got no idee' where to pull off—"

Mr. Rutherford is wearing the type of smile that I think is called "bemused" as he watches Bobby's hands gesture widely over the state of Ohio. I pause by my front end and take in the show. Some old-time comedy.

Bobby glances up at me, says, "Keys're on the seat, Darlin'. Yer turn to drive."

Okay.

While I'm stashing the bags of drinks and snacks on the back seat, I become aware of some quick movements over by their side of the car. I guess you could call it a scuffle. Nothing all that major. Nobody cried out, nor even spoke a word far as I heard.

I left them to it, not knowing exactly what Bobby may have discussed with the gentleman before I came out. Maybe they had an agreement of some kind between them? Sounds far-fetched in hindsight, true enough. But what did I know? Bobby would bestow information in his own good time, like you may of gathered.

I take my keys off the driver's seat, get in, and prepare to start the car.

The front passenger door jerks open. I see both men move into the gap. Bobby appears to be urging Mr. Rutherford to get in. No rough stuff. Then the rear door opens. Bobby is sort of reaching overtop to maneuver the old man. Before I've quite decoded this weird dance, Rutherford is sitting in the front seat next to me. His door slams. Bobby swings in the back. He's leaning up close to the man. Slams his own door shut.

Right about here is where I first become aware of the knife. It's in Bobby's left, the hand closer to me. It occurs to me that he is left-handed, after all. Hadn't thought about that before. The knife comes to rest against the left side of Mr. Rutherford's neck.

Yes, I may of noticed earlier that Bobby had a knife in his possession. Maybe it was in his back pocket. I'm not sure. I don't believe he was wearing a belt. Back at my house, I may of felt the knife when he roughhoused me and hugged me, there against the wall, like he did. When I hugged him back, I may of noticed a knife.

I thought nothing of it. Well, why would I ask him about having a knife? A lot of men carry weapons, now don't they? I was glad he didn't appear to have a gun. Being out of prison and still "under supervision," that would of concerned me more. Don't you think?

I honestly don't recall exactly what type of knife it was.

Yes, later on, I did handle it. Yes—okay, it was a folding knife. Could of been a hunting-type of knife. Hunting was always big in their family, but I'm no specialist in the different varieties. It was about yay-long, say, nine inches opened up. Nice polished wood handle. Black-brown. Curved silver blade.

No, Mr. Rutherford did not yell or call out to anyone. Not at any time in or around the car. He did not appeal to me for assistance. There may of been other people about, at the gas pump or pulling into the parking lot—off a ways, like that.

I don't recall for certain.

Well, how could Mr. Rutherford sound distressed when he didn't say anything? No—I didn't hear any gasping or sobbing. Not a peep from him.

Yes, if he had yelled or said something, I might of caught on to "the seriousness" of the situation a little faster. Things might of gone a different way right there. I agree, that would of been better for everyone, all around.

Keep in mind, though, even when I saw the knife, even though Bobby had it up the old man's neck—

Well, no, wait—

I don't think I saw it *on his neck* till later. After I was already driving. But even if I did—keep in mind, I've never seen anybody held at knifepoint before. I don't know what to expect. How a person might act. I mean, I was going along with whatever Bobby had in mind, why wouldn't Mr. Rutherford do the same, so far as I knew?

Honest to God, I thought Bobby was pulling some harmless scam. A practical joke like he'd got me to pull on Mrs. O'Brien, taking her for ten bucks. Just a pointless little back-atcha. Like, "Us dumb hicks need a smart man's help readin' thisayere map, or readin' some official-lookin' letter we got back home. Cain't you come help us out readin' of it? Aw please, sir, c'mon."

Some shit like that. Probably it did start out that way. I feel certain that Bobby was not looking too far ahead to where things might realistically go.

So I began backing out of the parking space.

Bobby told me to wait a second. He opened the car door and grabbed the shopping bags. Mr. Rutherford must of set them down when the two of them were talking. Or maybe he dropped them. I think Bobby also retrieved my state of Ohio map off the ground.

I proceeded to turn and pull out of the Speedway—

Yes, at that point, about when I pulled back onto Highway 60, I heard Bobby say, "Don't you move now!"

His voice did sound harsh. It surprised me because, till then, he was using the dumb-hick voice that made me think a joke was in play. I glanced over, and I think that's when I saw the knife pressed against Mr. Rutherford's neck.

But just because some level of force is involved don't mean a man's got bad intent. Not deep down, not a man like Bobby. If he can't trick you into fretting a little bit, the joke's not funny—it can still turn out harmless in the end. So as I got up to speed on the highway, I still believed this would all be revealed as some funny ha-ha.

Bursts of heat lightning followed us out of town.

I drove past the turn to my folks' house in Devola. Bobby didn't say a word about it. Maybe that relief distracted me— at least our sneak attack on my dad was off the table for now.

Yes, along the way, Mr. Rutherford did speak up. Once or twice, he did. So you *have* talked to Mr. Rutherford—or your partners talked to him? He told you how I tried to protect him, right?

Fine. So you'll ask the questions.

No, Mr. Rutherford made no attempt to escape. Bobby might have flipped the child-safety locks on my car. It's possible the old man tried to open the door but couldn't. I didn't notice.

He never did shout, nor beg to be released. He did talk a little. I think it was after Bobby told me to take the exit for Highway 83. First he said, "Now, son, I don't know where we're headed, but I've got folks expecting me at home. They'll be wondering where I'm at by now."

He didn't sound terrified. I wouldn't say so. Just matter-of-fact, pointing out the obvious. Maybe he was clinging to his dignity for all he's worth, but the strain didn't sound in his voice.

Bobby said, "Never hurts to wonder. So long's you don't let it cloud your whole mind."

A couple minutes later, Mr. Rutherford tried again. Something like, "Is this personal for you two? Do I know you from around here?"

Or maybe he said, "You're not from out of town, after all, are you? Did I know you at the high school?"

I looked in the rearview then, to see Bobby's expression. Seemed to me we'd been made. Time to crack the joke. Claim no hard feelings, drop Mr. Rutherford back at his car.

But Bobby's face had gotten a hard look, even though he grinned when he leaned forward. He might of pressed the knife. I don't know. I was focused on driving.

Bobby said, "Don't fret, old man. We're gonna tell you all about it."

I know you don't care, but like I mentioned, my Great-Grandma Dorothy Howell lived out Duck Creek Road north of Whipple. She passed about eight-ten years ago. It was a sweet little white house with cobalt-blue trim. We helped paint it one time when I was little. The house has a deep porch across the front, screened in, and a six-pane gable, square above the front door. Off the back, there used to be a nice sleeping porch above something called a summer kitchen that burned some time ago.

"Here, up ahead—" Bobby told me. "Take the stone road."

Now I had a pretty good idea we were headed to Gramma Dot's house. What state it might be in since our foremother passed and the place changed hands, I hated to think.

Slowing down on the gray stretch of gravel, I looked out through the catalpas and mulberry trees that line the creek. I had turned on the headlights by now, but there was still enough glow in the sky, you could see the front rolling up from the south. A dark mass of cloud, so tall I thought it must reach outer space. It was coming on at a perceptible pace with flashes of light inside. It would be upon us any minute.

We passed a shrubby thicket tight by the roadside. Little birds flushed out in a flock. Right then, the heat lightening sharpened into forks. I saw the hard streak of light from one side of my windshield to the other. It looked like those birds swarmed over my car—almost like their bones cast shadows through their wings.

Past the last porchlight, I slowed down some more. You couldn't see much outside the tunnel of light straight ahead on the road, and I wasn't sure where to turn. Bobby leaned toward me and pointed between the front seats. So he must of put the knife down by then.

Bobby said, "There, girl. See it?"

The farm road had grass down the middle now. It slapped at my undercarriage. Even before my headlights caught it, I could just make out the shape of the house and the tree beside it, a big old sycamore. Loose leaves were blowing off it in the wind. I pulled up close, killed the engine. I left the lights on to shine at the side door.

Bobby got right out. He whipped the front door open.

"Here we are, Ol' Pal," he said. He used some such nickname. It sounded friendly enough. "Welcome to the humble abode."

Mr. Rutherford didn't move right away. I wasn't watching him. I had shook my hair forward, actually. Feeling shy to think he might recognize me. Okay, yes, I felt a bit ashamed, embarrassed. But I could tell the man was casting his eyes about, trying to get his bearings. After a couple seconds, Bobby took his upper arm and hustled him along towards the house.

I stepped out, left my door hang, leaned against my car. I was feeling kind of stranded, so I just waited there a minute, sizing up the old place. The porch screens were ragged, roof looked crumbly. I did notice Bobby kind of shoving the old man up the side steps. Had one arm twisted up behind his back.

I'd say his demeanor was jovial, like with the nickname. Light-hearted, in a way. But yes, I guess it had got to be menacing at the same time. That was becoming clear to me.

Yes, I believe Mr. Rutherford tried appealing to reason again. He said something like, *Why? I don't see what we're doing here. At least let me call my folks. They'll be worried—*

Those types of things.

The side door was not locked. I remembered that it opens to the kitchen, the regular kitchen. The screen door was off completely—it was leaning over by the sycamore tree. Bobby gave the wood door a shove with his flat hand.

Just before he went inside, Bobby remembered me. Looked over his shoulder and called, "Give me a minute then kill those headlights. And bring in the drinks, Darlin'. We'll be needing refreshments."

The sky had gone flat as a paving stone and hung low above me. For sure it was already raining back in town, but the thunder—barely noticeable before—still sounded distant.

Past the old handpump, gray and rusty, there was a lone picnic bench under the tree. I waded to it through overgrown grass, too tall by town standards but not so tall as a lawn neglected all summer. Also under the tree, I spied a sorry-looking push mower with semi-fresh grass coating the wheels. I remembered one of my brother-in-laws saying you had to keep country places mowed these days, whether anyone stayed there or not. Otherwise meth cooks would move right in.

I sat down on the bench, wished I had a sweatshirt, something to wrap up in. The wind was still gusting, and the sycamore tossed its mane like a restive horse. But I didn't want to go inside. It crossed my mind to get back in the car and beat it out of there. But, of course, Bobby would hear the engine start up. He would come to the door, maybe come right on outside. Flag me down. Ask where the hell I was going.

And also I thought of Mr. Rutherford. I knew I shouldn't leave him behind.

So I just sat for a minute.

Yes, I had figured out that things were headed in a bad way. The sight of Bobby pushing the old man up those steps and into a dark house is what clinched it. Till then there was still some benefit of the doubt.

My headlights showed where the back of the house was scarred from the fire. Charred uprights and frame of the old sleeping porch had been pulled down and piled off a short ways in the meadow. At the former rear wall of the house, a dozen rows of blackened chimney rock stood over heaps of collapsed rubble. The former doorway to the intact portion was covered with new-looking plywood.

Things had definitely gone south since the old place had
its heyday. I wondered if bats were roosting in the attic where
the high rear window was busted out. But evidently, Bobby
was caretaking a bit, here and there. Or so I wanted to think.

Was I afraid of him, my own long-favorite cousin? That's
hard to say, exactly.

I knew he would never harm me, certainly not if I kept on
his good side. That's where I wanted to be, for sure.

When fat drops of rain began to smack the sycamore
leaves, I knew my time-out was up. From my car I fetched the
shopping bags, killed the headlights. Found a corduroy jacket
in my trunk and slipped it on.

The side door swung shut behind me. In the kitchen, I stopped
for a minute, tried to get used to an eerie bluish light coming
from the front room. It was somehow dim but kind of bright
at the same time. From that light in the doorway I could see a
cardboard box-lid on the drainboard by the kitchen sink. It held
some dishes and pans, a makeshift drying rack. The sink itself
was nearly full of wrappings—MacDonald's, Taco Bell, Kettle
Corn, Wonder bread. Cupboards stood open, mostly empty, and
the old gas four-burner was crusted with God knows what.

I heard Bobby's voice. "Yo, cuz. C'mon in here.
Everybody's thirsty."

I stepped into the shadow of the doorframe and saw that
he'd put Mr. Rutherford in the corner of a large couch. The
old man resembled a gaunt shrub blown up there by the wind,
which set up a roar in the broken windows and many crevices
of the old house. I have to admit, he did not look good.

A camp lantern on an old gate-leg table in the middle of
the room was making that strange light. For a living room,
everything appeared random, an assortment of household
goods shuffled and dropped by a tornado. There were a couple of torn dinette chairs, one facing the far corner, like a kid's

punishment seat, and one opposite the decent-looking plaid davenport where the old man sat. That davenport was definitely the newest-looking item in the room. Its pleated skirt grazed the tracked-up linoleum floor. Stuff lay scattered all around it— an open duffle with crumpled laundry, pair of dirty boots, a tall table lamp on the floor near a wall outlet but not plugged in.

"We need you, Darlin'," Bobby said. "Our friend here could use a drink."

It did not appear to me as if Mr. Rutherford was injured in any way. I saw no bruises, no redness on his face, no clutching himself in pain or any such thing. But he did have a worried look on his face.

Yes, at this point I'll admit he looked scared.

I put the plastic bags with our Speedway loot on the table, where I also noticed Bobby had set down his knife, now folded in. I purposely covered it up with the drink bag.

Bobby zeroed in on the cigarettes. He tore the pack open right quick, lit up, and blew out his first drag. Then he lifted two Little Kings in one hand, passed one to me and opened his own. He tossed the cap in the general direction of the kitchen doorway.

I set my bottle back on the table and took an Arizona tea over to Mr. Rutherford. I opened and handed it to him. He took a long drink.

He may of said, "Thank you," real quiet. I think he did.

Right about then, thunder boomed directly on top of us. It made me jump. There was maybe ten seconds of Nature holding its breath before the downpour hit so hard it felt like the little house might topple off of its blocks and wash on down to the creek.

I wondered how bad the place might leak. Looking around, I realized the lightning flashes outside barely showed because the windows were covered with aluminum foil.

Bobby bent down toward the old man and amazed me, for one, by coming off with a Bible verse. He recited, *"When he speaks in thunder, the heavens roar with rain. He causes clouds to cover the earth. He sends lightning in the rain and releases the wind from his storehouse."*

I take a couple of bottles and step away to the corner of the room that is farthest from the lantern. Here, I am slightly behind that davenport, which stands almost in the middle of the floor. Twisting the top, I down a mini-vodka and chase it with the cold ale. I did that for my nerves. I start a line of trash on the windowsill: one mini-bottle, two caps.

Bobby delivered the Bible quote in melodrama style, like some grand old-time movie, but now he sits down on the dinette chair and says in a normal voice, kind of jokey again, "Ain't that right, sir? Ain't that what the Good Book says?"

He drains his Little King, reaches for another. Turns and tosses the cap. From the sound, it nestled into the trash pile in the sink.

"Y'see, Mr. Rutherford, the Devil can quote Scripture. You know that—you must of heard him quote many times. That zero-tolerance shit you laid down, that was all about 'Respect the elders,' and 'proper authority,' ix-nay on the 'Defiance disorders,' and blah-dee-blah. B'cause authority's ordained by God, right? Zero tolerance on disruption. Zero on dope. Zero left, zero right. Got me expelled so quick my head spun right-round! I tried to tell you, Sir. Didn't I say, 'You're a genteel sort, Mr. Principal. You don't understand our ways—I cannot allow no football star, no doctor's son, nor anybody to mock and disrespect me at this school. That could, seriously, lead to my great harm in life. Blood in the water, and sharks will be drawn. I cannot allow that.'

"My own dear daddy would of whupped me if I allowed that! What's a kid to do between the rock and the hard place?

But you came down on me, zero-toleratin'."

Bobby swings a thumb over his shoulder like an umpire. "I'm out. But how about those kids I's fighting with? How's come they didn't get expelled? Detention for them—just horsing around with their buds before sports team practice! While I get the boot, permanent."

This rant has the ring of welling up from some long-buried source. Some well-aged memory presumably based on fact. I never knew Bobby had such skills for speech and debate. At the same time, while I'm listening, I can't believe Bobby is dragging up this kind of shit from the ancient past. Like, does it matter which water flowed under what particular bridge that far back?

Mr. Rutherford tries to speak up, call him on it. "Son, whatever you're talking about must've happened 20 years ago, if it happened at all."

Maybe not the best tack. Bobby's not having it.

"*If it happened*? Like your memory's lapsin', or what? 'This kid's fightin', he's bustin' heads. Out on his ass!' Did you pause to consider, 'Could he be medicatin' hisself with these drugs, do ya think?' Nah! Why trouble yerself with questions? Nothin' about anger issues. Nothing like, 'Hmm! Maybe he's actin' out a real problem. Maybe it's what he learned at home—his dad beatin' on his momma, whupping the kids, fightin' the world.' Was I flowin' into a prison pipeline? Cause it was all about obedience, for you, right? Toe the line! Shut your smart mouth and march, kid—"

This line of talk flies out of the blue. Normally, I'd say the Howells are non-complaining people. Especially our Twist-line men—they do the deed, right or wrong. Don't bother justifying. And I sure never heard of Big Bobby beating on Aunt Sue. I wonder if that could be factual? In my childhood, kids got disciplined for sure when they deserved it. But wives were partners. Mostly off-limits for Howell men. So far as I knew.

But more than that—Bobby never seemed the type to blame his family or blame the world. It's like he's taking a jab with every notion that strays through his head. Random associations. For a minute there, I swear to God it reminded me of a comedy routine, except the punch lines were sad instead of funny.

Like, *How many white-trash punks does it take to screw in a lightbulb? Just the way they come: A dime a dozen.*

And he's not near done. Now he's up pacing the floor.

"Year after year, boys of Washington County—off to Iraq. But military ain't a great option if you've already displayed a rule-following problem, now is it? Recruiter was beggin' for warm bodies. Even takin' girls! But they didn't want yours truly." Bobby gives one scoff of a laugh. He blows smoke, drops his butt, grinds it on the linoleum. "I'm well aware—I ain't no prize. That's been made clear to me. But then my dad gets sent to jail. Comes home, has a stroke. What am I suppose to do?"

Mr. Rutherford lifts a hand of appeal from his lap. "There's a fund at our church," he says. "Social needs. We help folks on hard times. I'd be happy to nominate your family."

"Yeah, I know. My momma got 1200 bucks in a fundraiser at our own church. Covered one baby toenail of my dad's medical bills. No doubt your church gots a bigger fund—"

Bobby pauses to light another cigarette, waves and tosses the wooden match.

"But you must surely know, Sir—people hate charity. Everybody knows that. So you gotta use yer wits. Boot-strap yer way in this world. I managed. Found a way to make a living off the Army, after all." He sits back down on the dinette chair, leans forward and drops his voice, confidential-like. He shakes a finger at the floor.

"See, I became a recruiter, my own self! Those boys coming home with the PTSD, with eyes, arms, nuts blowed off from those IEDs—I became their provider. Plenty of their parents, too. Not to mention wives, girlfriends, kids comin' up. 'Course it was the doctors with medical plaques on the wall got 'em started. Guys like me just kept 'em going, long as they could go. I covered overflow demand. People need relief, Mr. Rutherford. Relief of pain, anxiety—those are human needs. I rounded such folks up, drove 'em to the 'pain clinic' by the busload.

"So some of them crazy desperate people decided to snort their pills instead of washing 'em down. Then they decided to shoot up. Was that my fault? I never stuck a needle in anybody's arm."

Again, Mr. Rutherford raises a hand. Both hands this time. "I know people at the Health Department. Good people. There's treatment programs. There's help to kick addictions—"

Bobby waves his smoke in Mr. Rutherford's face. "I'm not some heroin junkie, old man. I'm addicted to cigarettes, so the hell what? Besides, I'm a lost cause." He puts a hand on his heart. "You got nothin' to fix me with. Nobody does. I ain't the one worth fixin'—"

I'm getting the drift of where Bobby's going with this. A sinking feeling grips my stomach. I may be hanging back, but there's really no escape from what's coming, what's going to happen. It's the same feeling like in our fifth-grade year's-end program, when I knew it was almost my turn to recite my poem. "Up the Airy Mountain," it was—

They stole little Brigette for seven years long.
When she came home again, her friends were all gone—

Bobby keeps at it. "The one you need to hear from, Mr. Rutherford, is this young lady over here. I've got yer typical bad-boy story. Nobody feels sorry for me. But she went through some real shit." He's on his feet now, waves his arm urging me forward.

I stay put, polish off my Little King. Maybe all the drinks are catching up to me. There's a drumming noise in my ears. Maybe the rain has gone from pouring to drizzle and back again a few times already.

Bobby carries on introducing me, like I'm going to put on a show. A big farce.

"Long days may of passed, but this girl's family was one that turned to you for help. Church-going folks—you know the type. And here their daughter, lands up pregnant sophomore year. Her parents came into your office. Consulted you, the education professional. Ain't that right?"

He looks over at me. I stay frozen.

The rain pours down again. *Like a cow pissin' on a flat rock,* my dad used to say.

"She got sent away on that smart advice you gave her family. Left school. Never to return. Saw some pretty sad shit go down. And what do you s'pose happened to that baby? After you sent her to off to prison-camp, she didn't even want to bring that child home."

It's a surreal experience. It honestly feels like I am watching Bobby on television. Like an actor on HBO, he stomps close to the old man and yells in his face.

"That's the kind of 'help' you handed out, motherfucker!"

No, it's not news to me that Mr. Rutherford referred my parents to the New Dawn Ministry. Nor that they took his suggestion, which may have been quite off-hand when it actually occurred. More on the lines of "This here's one type of option," than "You should definitely send your daughter *to this exact place.*" I've known all along the idea originated in the high school office and, frankly, I could care less. We were not a "wired" type of family. Never got the Wifi at home or any of that. And Momma wouldn't of gone to the library to google youth rehabilitation programs, even if she knew that term. Ask Jeeves, "Troubled Child—Pregnant 15-year-old—What to do?" Yeah, right.

So when the school principal happened to have a brochure—the same one I wound up passing out in churches when I toured with the Sweet Rebekahs—why, Momma would naturally accept that this godsend was the perfect place for her inconvenient daughter.

It is a small revelation to hear that the detail of Mr. Rutherford's role has been no secret to Bobby since God knows when. But I guess I need to get used to my business being public domain for anybody Momma ever poured out her heart to.

I shuffle out from the corner, lift another shot and ale from the bag on the table, and commence to knock those back.

Bobby is shaking out the contents of a capsule onto the back of his hand, snorts it up hard and quick. I'm hoping it's a Xanax. Might slow him down some.

When I get focused again, Mr. Rutherford is talking. His voice sounds energized, not as pathetic as before. He has rallied to his own defense.

"I tried my level best, believe me. Parents came to me every week, most of them at wits' end. We had kids hooked on crack, methamphetamine. Some had stolen from their own families to pay for this poison. They stole credit cards, ran up bills their parents couldn't pay. They'd buy tool kits, electronics, jewelry—anything the kid thought he could sell to buy more drugs—"

Bobby scoffs. "Any kid fool enough to rob his own family deserves to go to jail. That's totally beside the point." He points at me. "This young lady never stole. Never abused no illegal substance."

Mr. Rutherford holds up his hands like he's about to grab his own head.

"What I'm saying is, families get desperate. Their kids need discipline in the worst way. I saw these rehab ranches—'bootcamps,' if you will—as one last hope. One chance before involving the law. So yes, I gave out some brochures. They had a good reputation. I assumed the parents would investigate. See if they offered good programs for their children."

"Yeah, yeah," Bobby says. "We know your side. I can play it in my sleep. You just shut it, now, and let this girl talk. She'll tell you what's really what."

* * *

THE CHEDDAR POPCORN CALLS TO ME. I rip open the bag and snarf a few handfuls, spill some on the floor. I offer the rest to Mr. Rutherford, who shakes his head. I set the bag beside him on the couch cushion.

He may of been relieved to see me step up instead of Bobby. But he still looks a caution. I sit on the dinette chair and hear myself start to talk.

"My family wanted it in the worst way—that baby I was carrying. It was to be their firstborn grandchild. The catch was, they wanted my sister to pass it off as hers. That could of worked, except—Well, it couldn't of worked. My sister was willing to take it, but no. I had a foresight of how things would be, and I realized I couldn't go along with it—watch my baby be raised in my family but not as my own? Of course, I couldn't provide a father. And the real father would be in that same boat as me, hearing talk, hearing whispers, keeping his mouth shut."

When I fall silent, Bobby asks, "So what'd you do, LaDene?"

Sure, he's pretty lit up from the pills, but the tone of his voice isn't all show for Mr. Rutherford. He's still interested. I believed he was.

He asks again, "How'd you end up telling your folks?"

"Never did tell 'em much," I said. "The bare minimum."

My shadow cast by the camper lamp raises a hand to my mouth, and I suck down another long draw of my Little King.

* * *

UNLIKELY AS IT SEEMED, I had the visiting nurse to thank.

Once a week, all us preg-girls would line up in the hall outside a small general-purpose room at the back of the big house. The nurse drove in from Butler to write down our weight on a chart, take our blood pressure, dole out vitamin pills, ask about our appetite and such. She was a stout woman of 45 years or so with curly dark hair going gray. She always wore the same old-fashioned white nurse dress and white shoes. Her eyes never smiled, and she didn't have a sweet word for anyone.

We called her Nurse Hatchet because of her sharp nose and chin. But when I asked her, she came through for me.

Sometime in March or so, about my sixth month, I asked how a girl should go about getting her baby adopted into another family. A nice family. I had hung back to the end of the line, so the other girls had already been dismissed.

For the first time, Nurse Hatchet's eyes seemed to focus on me. She asked if that's what I was thinking to do.

I said, Yes, I was very sure about it.

She offered to bring me information from a social service agency. Told me they screen the families thoroughly to be sure they can provide a good home. Other girls here at The Ministry who gave up their babies had gone through this agency. It had a good record.

Hard as it was for me to admit out loud, I said, "My parents back home want to keep the baby in our family, with my sister as mom. I don't agree."

The nurse gave me a squinty look, like she knew this was only part of the story.

I said, "They want it raised by her and her husband. I'll be the aunt."

She said, "Such arrangements can work out well. But only if you supported it, gave your formal consent. No one can legally force you."

On the other hand, if I went with the agency, I could consider which parents I would like for my baby to have. I could choose among applicants "on the basis of educational background, employment, other children in the home, and those types of factors."

I nodded for what felt like a full minute.

She promised to bring along a social worker on one of her future visits to discuss "the process" with me. If I stuck to my decision, this social worker would assist me with everything needing to be done.

It sounded almost too good to be true. I couldn't help smiling. When I said, "Good," Nurse Hatchet actually leaned her head toward me and touched my arm.

Her eyes warmed up for a second. She said, "You do have to think of yourself in all this. Your wishes will be respected."

Then she turned down the hall to the front of the house. I could hear her rustle into a coat and close the big door as she went outside.

Someone would help me. I could look over "the factors" and choose the parents I liked. On a chair in the hall outside the room that passed for our medical office, I sat down, took a breather. No one was around on the ground floor of the big house, although I detected the telltale creak of Mr. or Mrs. Fitzsimmons moving about upstairs.

I sat resting and cherished the light-headed sense that someone would give advice and help me get my way for once. But still I wondered who could help break the news to Momma.

* * *

I HAVE TO ADMIT, being a Sweet Rebekah was a nice experience for me—that's the traveling music group that put on shows at small-town churches to spread the word about The Ministry and take donations. I heard that some families earned a discount or reimbursement of fees by letting their daughters tour and perform. Since Bernard O'Brien's father had paid my expenses, that didn't apply to me. But even without that, there were plenty of perks.

By joining, I became part of an elite. Trustees were tired old women. Elders had been beat on as inmates, and now they beat others. They pretended to care about morality, when in fact they were just a half-step over the line from delinquents their own selves. But the Sweet Rebekahs rose above the crowd by virtue of God-given talent and good behavior. If anybody at The Ministry had managed to get a handle on that gift of "self-control," it was us. And everybody recognized, we had something to aspire to.

Before I got put in the group, I was seen as a more or less clean-nosed nobody who palled around with that notorious queer, Annalee. Now I was special. If I hadn't come into that position where I had a little self-respect, I don't know how I would of got up the courage to defy my momma and insist on giving my baby to strangers.

I don't claim that I'm any great musical talent. I've just always been able to harmonize. Other girls had prettier voices than me, but it's not so easy to hear an old familiar melody right in your ear, when you have to sing different notes entirely for the alto line or what have you. I was in the second soprano section, which is sometimes like melody—just a wee bit off. Or other times, it's totally different. Very tricky. But I'd sung before in youth choir back home so I knew how to shut down my ears and expectations and stick to my own note.

The Sweet Rebekahs pulled together as a group. We were not necessarily close friends, and did not necessarily trust each other, but we could cooperate for the sake of a project that we were all part of. Some were true believers in the Word of God. They accepted that our solemn mission was to inspire donations to The Ministry. The rest accepted that this was the ticket to a cushier deal than we'd been getting. I might of been one of the first type when I arrived in Missouri, but by the time I got into the group, I was definitely one of the second. We were not critics, of course, but we admitted in private that not all the methods employed in the program were really proper from a humane standpoint.

While I was still pregnant, I did not perform with the group. I was memorizing the songs, getting into practice. Although, actually, it might of been possible for me to perform, and I happen to know our music director considered taking me on the May tour, in my eighth month.

Mr. Dyson was a slender gentleman with wavy chestnut-brown hair combed in a side part like some English actor. He always wore a brown suit with black pinstripes—part of his overall color scheme—and pastel-blue shirts. He had a whole collection of silky-looking ties with exotic prints on them like draperies in a fancy house. Many girls whispered that he was a homosexual. It's true his manners were on the prissy side, but I think they were mainly guessing at why the Fitzes trusted him in our midst.

He put it to me like this about the tour—"It should be perfectly safe for you to come along. Your due date isn't for another six weeks. But even in the event of unexpected developments, we would never be in such a remote locale that we couldn't get you to a hospital, should need arise."

Of course, I wanted to go out traveling, and I didn't know enough to fret about being far from a hospital. But there was a major catch—

"Audiences will need some explanation of your condition," Mr. Dyson went on. "You would need to give a three-to-five-minute speech. Very simple—it wouldn't have to divulge personal details or elaborate on your emotions. You made a mistake, failed to wait for marriage, period: End of story. The main focus would be your refusal to have an abortion. It could be very powerful."

The testimonial.

I said no, but I gave my promise to stay with The Ministry after my delivery to tour with the group. So long as I would not be required to speak.

Truth was, I'd had regrets about that whole abortion question. Since my baby started kicking, of course, I loved her like a real person. (Or him. I never knew which it was until she finally came out). But the honest truth is, I would of aborted her in a second before she started moving, if only it had occurred to me back in Ohio, before it got too late. And I've always believed that would of been for the best, in a lot of ways.

I'm well aware that sounds despicable—that I wish I could of killed my child before she became my child. But that's how things change in time's unfolding. What's true at one moment turns out different later on. It's something I can't help.

So my "testimonial" would of been a lie, even if I wasn't deathly afraid of speaking in front of people.

The morning of June 5 dawned early, like every other. I got up, washed and dressed, knelt for prayers, went to breakfast, and went out for exercise with three pregnant girls who had come to The Ministry after me. Mrs. Virland was off that day, I don't know why. Maxwell, one of my bunkhouse elders, decided I could be in charge of our walking group. She sent us off on our own.

I took the loop clockwise, starting toward the big house and the now-deserted puppy shed. It was a beautiful morning, full of sunshine but still cool and fresh, the fields green, air sweet. Something was in bloom off somewhere nearby, maybe roses over in Mrs. Virland's yard. She had talked about them and promised to cut and bring some to show us. The Peace Rose, she said, was the loveliest.

We rounded the corner behind the garage. Lacy white wildflowers were blooming along the fence. There's the garden patch, full of pale-orange zucchini blossoms. Tomatoes coming along, covered with yellow-star flowers, tied to their creosote stakes.

The girl next to me is seventeen years old. She's got blue eyes and a short, gold-brown ponytail. I suppose she's nice, but haven't learned her name. Her baby bump has barely started to show.

She's asking me, "Does the nurse make you take those special vitamins? I hate taking pills. And those things are big as horse honkers. Real hard to swallow—"

Right before we come abreast of the dining hall, I'm thinking what to say to this. Yes, I take the vitamins; seems like a good idea, considering the food we get is not so fresh. But the answer I mean to give flies out of my head. Not quite meaning to, I stop in my tracks.

The girl behind keeps coming. She bumps into me. "Whoa—sorry!" she hollers. "What's going on?"

A flood is pouring down my legs, over my socks, into my shoes. It gives off an odor. About how I imagine the Gulf of Mexico might smell on a hot summer day. The round ball of my belly feels like it's trying to pull in tighter, like it might actually cramp down smaller, instead of continually growing.

The three girls gather round me.

The seventeen-year-old's blue eyes get big. She looks from my soaked feet to my face. She says, "That's your water breaking. You have to go to the hospital."

I just look at her, not ready to speak while my insides tighten and pull.

"Are you in labor?" asks the freckle-faced redhead who bumped me. "What does it feel like?"

"Count the seconds between the pains. The doctor's gonna ask how many." This from the third girl, dark-eyed with a bandana on her head.

I can't count seconds because I don't feel anything except this weird pressure in my gut, like all the baby's muscles are tensing at once. Like maybe he's braced his feet on my lower ribs and wants to force his head down between my legs. I feel an urge to sit. Or squat down. Maybe I need the toilet. Rarely did I stroke my belly like pregnant ladies do in movies, but I cradle it now, bending over.

Then it hits. A knife probing through my intestines. From the top layer, deeper and deeper. A tight shriek comes out of me.

The two young girls take my arms.

The older one says again, "They have to take you to the hospital. When your water breaks, you could get infected."

"Go to the big house." I gasp a shallow breath. "Ring the bell till someone comes down."

Seventeen lopes off on long legs. The young ones hold onto me. We shuffle toward a wooden bench that lately appeared by the vegetable garden. After four tiny steps I have to stop. The knife stabs again. A whimper rises up against my will.

"Count the seconds," the bandana girl insists. "It's important. And it'll distract you."

But the pain lacks any start or stopping point. It lets up slightly, lingers on a low boil, and ramps up again before it ever ended. It grapples around my whole body, knees to boobs. Front to back. Like my skin is crawling in red-hot wavy lines.

I scream. Nothing can distract from this. Screaming seems like a mirror of the pain. Puts it outside of me, but then it's everywhere, all around me. That almost makes it worse. But keeping quiet is impossible.

The little redhead says, "They'll give you something at the hospital. Something for the pain." She looks to the bandana girl. "They'll give her something, right?"

I can see she's hoping for a comforting answer. She looks scared. I can't get a word out, but I take a few more steps.

They get me to the bench. For some reason, I can't turn around. No longer do I want to sit. I brace my hands on the back of the bench, raise one knee to the seat. For a second this lean delivers relief. I catch a breath, drop my head.

"I'll count the seconds for you. Just give me a sign when to start."

I give this stubborn girl a hard look—focus on her long lashes, bright complexion.

She takes this as the sign and starts to count, "One, one-thousand. Two, one-thousand. Three, one-thousand. Four—"

The knife takes me again, cuts into my tender parts. Divides my stomach from my liver from my lungs. Squeezes each part in its own separate vise.

I scream, sob. Is it God's plan to rip me apart? Is this my reward for not aborting? Why have you abandoned me?

"We should pray," the redhead says.

I hear a door slam. Sounds like the big house. With great effort, I turn to look. My tall girl is running back to us. I hear her call out some optimistic words.

Behind her, Mr. Fitzsimmons walks briskly in the direction of the garage.

"That's right," I whisper. "Get on your knees and pray for me right here. Mr. Fitz'll love that."

It seemed like forever since I rode in a car.

When Mr. Fitz pulls up in his big white Lincoln, I remember how his wife picked me up from the bus stop in Rich Hill all those months ago. How JoBeth played the responsible older sister, my supervisor. I stumble toward the door, my helpers on either side. Behind the wheel, Mr. Fitz is grinning, spouting off about blessings and praise. I don't know whether to try sitting or lying down on the seat. After another long freeze-up of pain, I wind up crouching in the back. The older girl tries to get a seatbelt around me, but I shove her away.

As the car rolls forward, I glance back at the "campus," the buildings, the three huddled girls. They do look truly concerned for me.

For the first few minutes, Mr. Fitzsimmons kept quoting Bible verses and insisting I should pray for the baby. Then he gave up and just concentrated on getting me to Bates County as fast as possible.

I had the social worker's card in my skirt pocket. I'd kept it with me every day the past month. It felt very special when Nurse Hatchett brought her out to meet with me. An elder came to find me on laundry duty, and I was excused from work to come sit in the little medical room for a private talk with the two of them. The social worker was young, maybe thirty, and pretty in a green dress and jacket. Her kind eyes and patient voice stayed with me after we talked, after I filled out and signed a ton of paperwork. The part that impressed me most was when she explained that "a colleague in Ohio" would take care of contacting the father for his "relinquishment of parental rights."

I suppose that procedure actually took place by mail, but the way I pictured it at the time, someone would go to the O'Brien home in person and do this "on my behalf."

At first, I had been reluctant to reveal Bernard's name, and of course, I had never heard those big words before, but soon I caught on to the gist of things. Bernard had never come to my house, but in my mind, this "colleague" would go right to his door and bang until someone opened up. She would talk to the head of the family, who was paying for everything, and she would demand the father's relinquishment of rights. I felt giddy, agreeing to this.

At the hospital, I gave the social worker's card to the nurse who rolled me in a wheelchair behind a door at the emergency ward.

She glanced at the card. "Oh, yes. We'll give them a call in good time."

"And I don't want that man back here," I said. "The man who brung me in."

"He won't come back," she promised.

It was strange that the pains receded as soon as I got inside the hospital. It no longer felt like I was being cut open. Just embarrassing that two different nurses kept looking and reaching inside me and talking amongst themselves. Even so, they were kind and tried to put me at ease.

When I told them my baby wasn't supposed to be due for another two weeks, the younger nurse said, "Each child keeps its own timetable." She said not to worry. She showed me how to breath, slow and deep.

It was a relief to be away from The Ministry. And it was good that the baby was coming early, on its own timetable. My momma had talked about driving out to be with me for the delivery. Now she wouldn't be able to get here in time. I knew she would of bent over backwards begging and convincing me to give the baby to Jo Beth.

But I hadn't changed my mind. I had viewed the factors online and picked out a couple in St. Louis to be my child's parents. They were in their late-thirties and had a red-brick house. The dad was a radiology doctor and mom a high school music teacher. He played in a basketball league, she played the violin. They had a six-year-old son but could not have more kids of their own. They attended a house of worship called Temple Beth El.

I was thinking they would want a girl, so that's what I was hoping for.

* * *

MY CONTRACTIONS DID NOT ADVANCE at a steady pace. In fact they seemed to stop altogether for long stretches at a time.

The nurse said I had an "inefficient labor."

A doctor stopped by and gave me some kind of shot with a scary long needle. It knocked me out for a nap that felt like many hours. But when I came to, the pain roared back with a vengeance. A rude awakening. That awful knife carved me up one side and down the other. I screamed—the nurse reminded me to think only of breathing and not to be afraid. No matter how bad the pain got, she promised I wouldn't die. That did help me relax a little. She had kept her promise not to let Mr. Fitz come near me, so I trusted her.

Back before I had fallen asleep, Mrs. Fitz did stop in. She acted all sweet and kept saying what a "momentous event" it was for me to be bringing a new soul into God's Kingdom. Of course, she also had to comment on my plans.

"I spoke with your mother on the phone," Mrs. Fitz said. "She insists that you should reconsider. Are you certain this adoption is what you want?"

Yes, I was certain. Momma had called three times before. Girls rarely got to talk with their families by phone, but for this, they made an exception. I had talked to Momma and also to sisters Jo Beth and even Effie. The latter, the eldest of us girls, shirked her duty and made scant effort to convince me to keep the baby in the family.

"You gotta do what's best for you," she said in her usual flat-tone voice. "I support whatever you decide. Probably best if we don't say much about it once you get home."

Jo Beth understood, too, or so I hoped. "It could only work if you're sincerely on board," she remarked, picking up on Momma's wording. Maybe she was actually relieved not to get stuck with twins. "Twins," that is—ha-ha. Momma had sworn to pick up all the slack, but still, it couldn't be a piece of cake. And think of all that money I was saving them.

But talking directly to Momma was the awfullest thing I ever went through up until my labor started. I hate to remember it, though every word stays with me.

"LaDene Faye Howell, that is my grandchild. Mine and your daddy's. You want to deny us that joy? He or she—it don't matter which—is our own blood. We already love that child from the bottom of our soul. Some things in life are bound to be hard. You have learned that now, I guess. I know it won't be easy to look on and keep a secret over long years. But it's meant to be for the best. For all of us. I know we can make it work. Together. Can't you grasp what I'm saying to you, LaDene?"

I could tell she was crying, even though her voice got harder and harder the longer she talked. I cried, too, and I could barely say anything for my voice shaking. Nothing I could think of was making any difference.

I wouldn't be able to stand it, Momma. I'd mess up, let the secret slip out. You keep saying that, but Jo Beth would lord it over me. You know she would.

My momma. Unshakable. Later on, I kept hoping she would forget about my baby once Jo Beth's arrived. And now, these many years later, my parents have got five grandkids from my two sisters put together.

But it feels like they never forgot.

After the agony of labor, giving birth was easy. They wheeled me into the brightest, lightest room in the world with dials and machinery on all sides. I pushed twice—really, it happened by itself, no active effort from me—and out slid baby. My little girl. My daughter. Her blue-looking eyes were wide open, her tiny arms waved about. She didn't cry, but I wouldn't let them hang her upside-down and slap her. After a second, she started breathing on her own just fine. She weighed five pounds and fifteen ounces.

When they wheeled me into another room, I got to hold my daughter for about one hour. The social worker had arrived by then, the same nice lady as before. She said holding the baby for a short while wouldn't hurt anything, but she seemed a bit nervous, checking her watch every few minutes. Looking back, I expect she was worried I'd fall in love and change my mind about giving her up.

My child was the only thing that existed in the world for that time. She looked around for about two minutes before she fell asleep, but I know she saw me, and I believe she had her own understanding of who I was and why we were together on that first day of her life.

At first, it made me sad that her tiny head and arms were so red, and I could do nothing about it. But I loved her perfect little face, and the bright red color seemed to cool down a little over our time together. I couldn't decide if her skin was more like wool felt or velvet. She had a headful of dark hair that the nurses had washed and slicked up in a cute little wave. I remembered that some girls had said heartburn during my pregnancy meant the baby was growing hair. So maybe that's one old tale with some basis in fact.

It seemed funny that the line of the baby's profile reminded me, totally out of the blue, of a few old photos Momma has of my dad when he was a boy. I hadn't laid eyes on those pictures in years, but they came right to mind when I saw my daughter. One picture shows Daddy leaning back in a tire swing at his folks' place outside Coal Run. His head is leaned back so the shape of his face shows clear against the barn in the background. So funny to see that same nose and chin on my little girl. He'd been a cute country boy in overalls and bare feet—now his first grandchild is a city girl, growing up three states away.

While she snoozed in my arms, I sang to her.

Dreamland opens here,
Sweep the dream path clear.
Little child, now listen well
What the tortoise may have to tell...

I gave her a secret name that I will never tell to anyone. It's only for me to know. She never nursed from my body. She was too sleepy to try. The nurse told me that going through labor wears them out, too.

When I kissed my baby good-bye, I thought I was happy for her. I knew I had picked the nicest family in all of Missouri. But before the social worker's shoes went quiet at the end of the hall, I was sobbing like they'd ripped the heart out of my chest. I didn't really stop crying for over a week.

The nurse gave me pills to keep the milk from coming in. She recommended a special tea. The doctor prescribed birth control, which was supposed to help my body get back to normal ("*Not* for going out and having sex again"—as Mrs. Fitz thought she needed to warn me). For a day and a half they kept me at the hospital and brought ice packs for my breasts.

I ate everything in sight, including all the sweets I could get my hands on. I was sore, miserable, lonely. I had lost my faith in God. Not that I didn't believe God exists, but looking

deep in my heart, and thinking about what I'd learned of this
world, I saw that He is nothing like a human being who I
might, now and then, reach out to or get help from. He is high
above and far away. If He cares about people—one by one, at
any rate—His signs for showing it are beyond understanding.
Cold comfort. If He cares at all, it must be like we're a huge
flock of birds that covers the sky. If a few get shot down before
their time, there's plenty more still winging along.

And even if we all end up going extinct, God's probably
okay with it. People are saying that more and more these days,
you know, like from a meteor hitting the earth or a world
war or other human stupidity: We had our chance, fucked it
up royal, now on to the next phase. No skin off God's ass!
Maybe that's what he had in mind all along. He can just go
back to the drawing board.

That's what I believe to this day.

* * *

SO NOW YOU'RE WONDERING, why did I loosen my tongue
about all this after so many years? There in Gramma Dot's
old parlor, reduced to a trashed-out campsite for my ex-con
cousin, why would I reveal myself and my feelings in front of
the very school official who played such a key but, basically,
off-hand role in what befell me? Was it to reproach and seek
revenge? C'mon, that's ridiculous. Mr. Rutherford didn't "get
me sent away" from home. My parents would of sent me to the
St. Louis Zoo if somebody they thought was a real "authority"
said it was the place to go. Nor did the old principal cross my
mind in making the decision not to attend school again after I
came back. I had bigger considerations to think about.

Did I share Bobby's anger? Anger at the world? I was not
thinking about that. I could see how miserable Mr. Rutherford
was feeling by then. He did drink some of the tea I gave him but

never touched any snacks and didn't really relax, even though he may of felt a little better when I started talking compared to Bobby. He probably figured I was less of a threat.

Yes, I'd say he was right about that. I was hoping we all could get out of this with a minimum of harm to any of us. I wanted to do what I could to make that happen.

* * *

LIKE I SAID BEFORE, I had been looking forward to touring with the Sweet Rebekahs. I'd promised myself that adventure. Most people might say, Going around a bunch of Midwest villages—that's a joke, not an adventure. But for me, it was a chance to see *something* different. Something beyond what I knew. And the main thing was, it put a distance between the adoption and going back to my family.

Our tours had one main goal—praising The Ministry in order to take in money. That goal had two parts: We had to show that we were ideal young ladies able to produce nice music, but we also had to remind people that, formerly, we'd been in sore need of reform. Our director, Mr. Dyson, was continually juggling the musical needs of the group against the testimonial skills that each of us might bring to the show. Not all girls were good at both, and we had high turnover— girls were going home all the time. After all, getting into the group in the first place meant you had displayed good behavior, so presumably, you were ready to graduate out.

That summer when I joined the tour, a couple girls came along who didn't sing at all. They just told dramatic stories of getting swept up in a bad crowd, taking drugs, getting kicked out of school—going over to the Devil's way, in short. One girl, her name was Kerrianne, could cry real tears every single time she told her story, and she could smile pretty, right through those tears, when she talked about finding Jesus, at last. Kerrianne was a genuine actress. She got more applause than anyone. I thought she must be at least partly sincere about it to make such a big impression, even though she would joke and shrug afterwards like the tears hadn't meant all that.

A typical tour lasted three to four weeks and covered a region like, say, eastern Kansas, hitting up to 15 churches. The ideal set-up was when we could perform twice on a Sunday at the same church. We'd do one song during the regular service—a "teaser"—and then a full-length show (about 80 minutes) after a fellowship dinner. That way, we collected money twice without extra driving. Those churches also had to put us up and feed everyone. Us girls usually bedded down on sleeping bags in a basement or right on the pews. Some helpful lady of the congregation would sleep on a cot or recliner to chaperone us through the night. Mr. Dyson and whichever of the Fitzes was traveling along at the time would stay in the home of a pastor or deacon.

Each girl had one khaki calf-length skirt that we were supposed to wear at all times when appearing in public. To keep those clean and nice, we wore thrift-store jeans for riding in the van and hanging around amongst ourselves between shows. We also had plain blue Oxford shirts and white blouses with ruffly collars.

In September, on my third tour, I got to perform in a special quartet. We sang "O Come, Angel Band" and "Gather by the River" in four-part harmony with hand gestures. A cappella—that's not easy. There's no extra pauses to catch a breath. I had got friendly with a girl named Samantha who stood on my left and sang the first alto line. Our voices blended real nice together. Sammy, as she invited me to call her, was from Ohio, like me—from Mt. Orab outside Cincinnati. She had turned eighteen in July but was staying in the group to earn the discount on what her parents paid to get her cured of pot-smoking and backtalk.

Sam was like me—hated testimonials. But she was so pretty, with wavy auburn hair and wide green eyes, and she was such a good singer that Mr. Dyson prized her in spite of her refusal to testify about the evils of marijuana. I, on the other hand, was getting pressure to come up with a speech for the show, particularly since three of our best talkers had lately bowed out and returned to their families.

For all her infuriating fakeness and vanity, I have to admit Mrs. Fitzsimmons was fair to me on this point. She never piled on the persuasion. Or maybe she just realized my reluctance would make me a piss-poor shill for those donations from the git-go. But on my third tour, Mr. Fitz traveled with us, instead. And he was unrelenting. He forced one shy girl named Florence to give a talk about how she turned to shoplifting to fund her pill habit, got caught, and spent three weeks in Juvenile Hall. I heard her struggle through this speech four times, and it never got any better. Anyone could see she was humiliated airing that dirty laundry in public.

One night when we rolled out our sleeping bags side by side on the basement floor where we were camping, I confessed to Sammy that Mr. Fitz was wearing me down.

"He won't take no for an answer. Just keeps coming back with more reasons why I ought to 'speak up."

"Yeah, I heard him in the van today," Sammy said. "That was out of line."

In front of everybody, Mr. Fitz had announced, "LaDene, you need to show some gratitude for all this growth in the spirit Our Lord has blessed you with. We have gone the extra mile to lift you up. Now you need to do your part. Don't disappoint me, girl."

Half the girls looked at me like I was growing devil-horns. And Kerrianne (the actress) chimed in with something like, "You *should* testify. It's not so bad. I can help you work it up."

And more bullshit on that line. Fitz was never so happy as when he could inspire peer pressure.

"I'd as soon cut my tongue out," I told Sammy.

"None of that." She punched my shoulder, but in a sweet way.

Sammy hadn't met Annalee, and I didn't like to talk about the nasty stuff my previous friend had gone through with Mr. Fitz. But it was a relief to know that my new friend understood how it made my skin crawl for him to demand the one thing I had put off-limits.

Turned out, Sammy had a solution to all my problems.

That tour was centered in southern Indiana. We did shows in Greensburg, Edinburgh, Lawrenceburg ("all the burgs," Florence said with an eyeroll), and too many smaller spots to keep track of. Everybody knew that Sammy was leaving us in Versailles to go back home to Ohio. We had half a dozen performances scheduled after that but would need to muddle through without her.

In the Friendship Community Church the night before Sammy's last show, Mr. Dyson sprang for a sheet cake that said "We'll Miss You, Samantha." The pastor of the church and his wife joined us for a toast with Hawaiian Punch. We sang a couple of teasers for the next day's show. Everyone was hugging Sammy and telling her to "Go with God! Keep sweet!" and such.

I was feeling like the world had been emptied out once more. Then, when she passed me an extra square of cake, Sammy whispered, "You want to come with us tomorrow? It's my boyfriend picking me up, not my parents. We can take you home. Ol' Fitz won't know till after you're gone."

My mouth gaped open. All I could do was nod.

"After the show tomorrow, be ready. Don't breathe a word." I threw my arms around her neck, dropping my cake to the floor in the process.

True, I could of planned with my family to go home any time in the months since the baby came. Momma had offered to send a bus ticket, or maybe somebody would actually take off work to come get me. But refusing to discuss the adoption left me in a kind of mental limbo. I was still weeks shy of my sixteenth birthday, but I had declared independence of a sort. I needed my family—and missed them much as ever—but I couldn't picture going back to the old terms of doing everything I was told.

I liked singing and riding around in the van, so I stuck with that for almost three months, longer than most other girls. Time flowed by. I sent home a postcard every week from somewhere along the road. Now, Sammy's offer seemed like my perfect solution. A chance to get away from Mr. Fitz and go home in my own way. Better yet, the prospect of pulling off an escapade filled me with a sense that I could figure out what the hell came next in my life.

All that proved true, in a way.

Sammy's boyfriend, Nolan, was a cute guy. Sandy-haired, real fit, about 25 years old. Said he was a welder from the city of Toledo, which sounded like big-leagues to me. Him and Sammy had met at a concert in Columbus, some music group I'd never heard of. He used his cell phone to play music over the car radio, too—lots of tunes I'd never heard, but most of which I liked just fine.

Our plan was simple, really. Out front of the Friendship Community Church, everybody gathered round Nolan's car, waving good-bye to Sammy after her last concert. I made sure Mr. Fitz saw me there, blowing kisses. Then I slipped through the crowd—a good-sized bunch of slow-moving senior citizens. In the fellowship hall, I dropped my skirt by the pile of rolled-up sleeping bags and left it behind. My jeans were already on underneath. Double-quick, I ducked out the rear door we had scoped beforehand. It opened on an alley that ran between big old-fashioned houses. I pulled it shut behind me with soft *click*. Pressed to the wall of the church, I barely drew breath, waiting for Sammy and Nolan to pull around from the street out front. So scared of getting caught and held back, I imagined every voice and footstep from inside the church was Fitz coming straight for me. It was probably thirty seconds, but seemed like eternity before the red Mustang turned up the alley—my saviors.

We flew out of that town at 70 miles an hour. A short ways down the road, Nolan pulled over and stopped. The young couple proceeded to make out for several minutes. Also, there was an item of business: Nolan wanted me to call Mr. Fitz and swear I had left of my own free will. He didn't appear super-worried, but didn't like the idea of getting charged with kidnapping, either.

I must of gone pure white at that proposition. The thought of speaking to Mr. Fitz was unbearable. He would demand that I return immediately. Also, I truly believed a phone call might help the cops or state troopers to locate us and grab me back—like they would instantly trace Nolan's cell phone, which—I had no idea how it worked.

Sammy came to the rescue again. She took the phone and dialed, those little number tones like perky finger-jabs in our oppressor's face. I guess she'd memorized the number for just this purpose.

After a minute, she began in an extra-low, nasally voice, "Well, good morning, Mr. Fitzsimmons. Or afternoon now, isn't it? I've been trying to reach you for hours—"

Nolan grinned at me, and I clapped hands over my mouth.

Sammy stated that she was Mrs. Verna Howell of Marietta, Ohio, mother of LaDene. (That was a slip-up—Mr. Fitz would of had my Devola address somewhere, but thank God, not before his eyes at that moment.)

"Well yes, I have been calling you all morning. Was your phone turned off? I need to notify you that my girl, LaDene, has full permission to ride home to us in the company of Samantha Woodside and Mr. Nolan Dupray." Except, that wasn't Nolan's real last name.

Sammy's incredible voice pulled it off. As my mother, she agreed to send in any necessary paperwork "by return post." I can't say if Fitz fell for the story or just decided not to risk calling the lady on the line an imposter.

Sammy rang off with a sweet, "God bless you and Mrs. Fitzsimmons. M'bye, now."

Nolan gave a loud whoop out the window. He honked a series of blasts on the horn and peeled out once again.

I hugged Sammy from the backseat, nearly laughing my head off. Then I swung my braid over my shoulder, slid off the rubber band, and started unbraiding till my hair was all loose. It seemed like the most important thing to do at the time. My scalp sighed with relief.

Up front, those two were drumming on the dashboard, singing a chorus like it was their old routine: "Freedom, freedom, freedom, freedom, FREE-DOM—"

A smart person, thinking things through, would of realized that we would stop at a motel along this trip, and anybody seeing how the two of them kissed, could of figured we'd stop sooner than later. Marietta was less than a day's drive, but once they dropped me at home, those lovebirds would be fresh out of excuses for not showing up at Sammy's parents' house in Mt. Orab.

They may not of needed me as the pretext, but I was handy to have along.

We came to a little motel on State Rt. 125, on the edge of Decatur. It was not too run down and had a cute old sign that said The Double Rainbow with multi-colored neon tubes arched across the top. We arrived well before the sign was turned on, though, around 3 o'clock in the afternoon.

Nolan pulled into the parking lot, turned to me, and explained that he needed some "rest." He hoped I wouldn't mind if we stopped here overnight. "We'll get you on home tomorrow," he promised.

"She doesn't mind," Sammy said. "Do you, LaDene? She gets it."

Of course, I was in no real rush to get home. I hadn't called ahead and didn't relish the prospect—feeling some dread of how I'd be greeted. But I also didn't have a red cent on me, nor anything but the clothes on my back. They knew that.

"Forget it," Nolan said. "It's on me." He got out and headed to the office beneath the Double Rainbow sign.

Sammy said, "We'll try and get you your own room. But if we need to share, you can give us a few hours of privacy, okay? Maybe visit that little library we passed? You'll have your own bed and everything, for sure."

You can imagine what the concept of privacy conjured up after living in bunkhouses with a dozen or more girls for the past eight months. Half a room to myself sounded like a super-delux hermit's cave.

September in southern Ohio is a green world glazed in sun-honey wrapped in sweet air. Nothing had been touched by fall so far, but every color filled my eyes like something fresh from the day of creation. We were in flat country along that road. Deep-green trees lined the horizon, and the bean field across the way glowed ripe and tawny with yellow butterflies flitting over top. The sky cupped everything in its bottomless dome. A caravan of clouds drifted by real slow to the south, so blinding white I could hardly keep my eyes on their shifting shapes—

A fox's tail, a puff-sleeve dress, an old man's bushy eyebrow, an empty grave.

Every door at that motel had one or two old lawn chairs on the side for relaxation. Ours also had a little metal table where Nolan set me up with refreshments—I had a bag of Fritos and a 20-ounce purple plastic cup filled with ice, sweet red wine, and something new to me that day: Popov's Vodka. I chose these from an array of supplies Nolan brought back from Russellville before him and Sammy dove into one of the beds in our room.

I had promised not to bother them for at least a few hours, and only after a special knock.

Across the road with rarely a car, I gazed on an old white Post Office building fronted with barrels of tomato-red geraniums and trailing vines. The bean field breathed softly in the breeze. A giant cottonwood by the last house on the side street cast deep shade on the crabgrass. All shapes of things looked clear and bright and restful—lazy creatures at home in the shelter of sunlight.

Air poured into my hungry lungs. Time ceased to scratch its tiresome ticking against a tally of emptiness. Instead, it rolled like unhurried waters into a waiting valley where, I believed in that moment, we all might live in a state of grace. No haste, no harassment, no laborious duties. These covenants were promised to all: The old collie dog that came round the house and flattened on her side beneath that cottonwood. A rusty-red squirrel that darted across the road and under a porch trellis, purple with climbing flowers. The black-flag dragonfly that buzzed up the pole of the motel porch roof and posed just three feet from where I sat drinking. After a minute poised in the sun, it spiraled down to rest on the concrete slab at my feet, wing-panes aglint.

Everything that had happened over the months when I must have been holding my breath, every sadness and regret, dropped away like scales from the blind man's eyes. Like a snakeskin that couldn't hold me any longer. All the worries of what I've done and would yet need to do, rise to my mind, sip air, and sink away—so many fingerling fish in a dim, cool pond.

Time enough to grow and fatten and get snagged on a hook.

For now, nothing matters but basking here as afternoon rolls into eternity. Sun flows under the awning, scorches the skin on that side of my face. I hear the rhythm of Sammy and Nolan behind the window. They are sharing a state of bliss in the rented room. He left me with a playlist of those weird songs he favors on his cell phone. I like listening to it, but the thrum of their lovemaking still comes through.

Sure, I envy them. The images they stir float over my own abandoned heart, my homeless love. Bernard whips through my mind, running a lap on the track back home, and off into the sunset. He was mine for an instant, one year ago this month.

Can that be possible? Another lifetime! A place and era that will never come again.

Momma slapping my face, sending me away.

Sister saying she killed her baby, but offering to take mine.

Whacks from a hard length of white pipe.

My best friend begging me to break her ankle.

Always keeping my head down.

As I suck on my delicious drink, those memories matter less and less. They lift up of their own accord and settle, nice and quiet, onto a shelf on a wall in a distant shed.

I lock it shut.

The light takes a sharper slant, still reaching for me, gilding my skin. What matters here is the surge of feelings coming home in my heart. A prodigal returned! The power of my pulse, my skin in the open air, my beating organs, my eyesight, freedom.

Nolan's playlist is a revelation. The songs lift me up, like I'm floating. One tune after another—they get into my blood.

Some new person inside me wants to go forth and take on the world, right the wrongs and slay the dragons. A new inkling of possibility grips my insides, it wants to get personal, get rough. Before I think about it, I'm on my feet dancing. I swing around the pole, twirl, sashay, jump over oil patches, bound off a bumper. My toes write poems in scattered gravel. My hair sweeps, unloosed from its captured braid.

Wind is rising in the cottonwood. At some point I notice I'm in the middle of the parking lot. I lean my head back and sing out loud. Not that I know the words—

Lead the way, Kingdom Come…!

My new life shines like summer sky:
I'm gonna be a headbanger, punk-rocker, teenybopper—

How, tell me how,
oh how, could I lose my mind?
Yesterday? Bless your soul!
Cast off dead time,
a life I used to own…

Take me down and lay me low, tell me something
no one knows…
None can alter
my true name,
None can falter
through my shame…

In a shining sky, no tether down,
when stars outrace
the speed of sound…
Touch me light as angels' hands,
never reach the ground…
Do we stand for nothin'

between the love and rage?
They told me you erased my name,
ripped out my sacred page...
I tread this wicked track,
there you go, fade on back.
I'll die ten-thousand times,
still there's a chain that binds...

Horses on the hoof, they'll trample down the lies.

They come to cleanse the earth, where your false
prophets hide...

A Mexican-looking man is standing off to my side, between two parked cars. His face is shy, but friendly. He talks to me in Spanish words (I guess that's the language). He uses a light voice. He seems to think I'll figure out whatever the hell he's saying.

Laughter coughs out of my mouth, but I let him come close. Maybe I give him a look, like I'd answer if I could.

My playlist has come to an end.

He holds out a hand, spins me in his arms. We're dancing! Some old-time cantina music comes rollicking out the open door of a motel room. The light inside is warm, pure yellow firelight.

Your skin, your bones, all yellow—
Lights lead you home, fade yellow—
No one is really gone...just hollow—
Ay yai yai yai yai—

I spin to a stop, clutching onto the pole of the porch roof. The wall, the chairs by the doors, roll to a stop. The honey color has melted out of the sky. It's gone dark blue—I remember that shade from art class. Something called "indigo." And over by the office, I see the rainbow sign! All lit up except for one section of red that must of leaked out its neon.

Pretty. They say Liz Taylor's eyes were violet. Most beautiful in the world.

The Mexican man is urging me toward the open doorway. Inviting, "escorting" me. He gestures like I should come inside and sit down for tea. A nice chat. He keeps saying things in his language. Seems like he's trying to ask me something. It's not pushy, not draggy. He's young. Nice-seeming. But I jerk back, pull my hand away, step away.

Over the highway, above the road light, bats are darting back and forth. Higher still, you can hear the voices of nightbirds. Shrill and freaky. One creature divebombs the Post Office—a shadow flashes. Which is our door, the door to Sammy and Nolan? I forget the room number.

When did all these cars pull in? Most rooms go by the week, they said. Harvest workers, construction crews. Little groups of men are hanging around by their cars, by their doors. Watching the drunk girl, of course. Guess I can't fault them for that. I've gone off on my own, asking for it. Anyone might rape me. Every bad thing is likely to befall me, putting my family to grief.

Finally, I spot my tall purple cup. On a rickety table by door number 12. Suck up some dregs, but basically, my cup is empty. I bang a bunch of times on the door. Can't remember the special knock. I try different knocks. A rhythm from those songs on the playlist. Hope I didn't lose Nolan's phone.

The Mexican-looking guy calls after me, calls me *Senorita*. He says, *Mi novia*— He gestures at his room, keeps smiling at me. From somewhere, he holds up a can of pop, like he wants to share it with me.

But our door cracks. Sammy opens an inch, slides off the chain, then opens wider. She's in a long T-shirt. Nolan's on the bed behind her, legs under the sheet. No shirt, but he pulls one on from the side table.

I make it across the room and crash onto the far bed. Did I go take a puke at the back of the parking lot? I sort of remember doing that, hope I won't need to do it again. Ought to drink some water, brush teeth. Sammy is talking to me. I say something back. My voice sounds normal, far as I can tell. She laughs, which makes me think things must be okay. Maybe I'm talking some semblance of sense.

She brings me a glass of water. Nolan will bring back hamburgers from town.

No, I don't want any burgers. But thanks. Soon I was dead to the world.

It was an afternoon, an evening, of blinding ecstasy—the time when I reclaimed my life. Magic moment of escape and delight that marked my forked path, such as it was. In the decade since that day, I've thought back to it more times than I can count. I've gotten pass-out drunk at least another 700 nights, though not one half so happy. At least I found my faithful partner. My best, unfailing friend.

* * *

AT GRAMMA DOT'S HOUSE, the hard rain has passed, but wind is still tossing drops off the trees. The lantern's soft hiss seems quieter, the circle of light smaller.

While I talked, it's like I barely saw the two men in the room—sinking so deep into my own story, reliving those long-gone days. Now, like I'm coming back to the present, I see that Bobby has pulled over the dinette chair that was off in the corner. He sits more or less between me and Mr. Rutherford, bent over, looking at the floor. All of our knees make a triangle, just a few feet apart from each other. Three people stuck in one room. How will we find our way out of this?

I see that the old man is focused on my face like he's watching some engrossing movie. That creeps me out a little.

A deep breath, then I say, "Hopefully, my family forgave me for giving up the baby. It's not something we revisit. After I got my apartment and moved out on my own, I think maybe they accepted how things would be. Seemed at first like that came as a surprise—like they had thought I'd be one of those maiden aunts of olden times, keeping house for them all my days, never taking a job. But I did finish school. Online, I did. Got work at the bakery with Effie. Got my nursing credential, and off I went. I think maybe then my parents decided to forgive me and love me as best they could, regardless of how things happened."

Trying to wrap this up, I say, "Hopefully, they did. I don't really know."

"Praise the Lord," Mr. Rutherford says.

Bobby's head, that had been slowly shaking while he stared at all of our feet on the floor, comes up a notch and angles toward the old man. His body rises from the chair. I see his hands tighten, fists forming.

Yes, that concerned me. But he didn't hit the old man.

"Did you hear what she said, you old fucker? She lost her faith in God. She thinks God don't even care if every last human goes the way of the dinosaurs. You know what that means for a country girl?"

Mr. Rutherford raises his eyes. His face is haggard like he's been out in the wind, but his eyes shine. He's actually almost smiling.

"I know she has hope. She carried on. And I know she is forgiven." Exhausted as he must of been by that time, the old man sounds energized by his own faith, his own optimism. But I remember thinking, this might not be the best way for him to go.

Speaking to me, he keeps it up, "You'll find your way back to the Lord, dear girl. You can if you want to. I'll pray on it. We can pray together."

"The fuck are you on about?" Bobby shifts to his back foot, cocks his head. He gives Mr. Rutherford a look like he's some wad of trash tossed on a nice lawn.

One of the empties next to Bobby's chair topples and rolls off along the uneven linoleum. Not that I was keeping close track before, but now I see that all the bottles I bought earlier have been drunk. They are all on the floor. And I see Bobby's pill collection lying open on the table, more depleted than it was.

This is not good. I know it full well. I've had more than enough alcohol for one day. It feels like sleep needs to be in my future, sooner than later. Instead, here we are in this mess.

Bobby says, "You don't hear a thing but the voice in yer own fuckin' head—"

Standing from my chair, I'm not sure what I have in mind till I realize I have to pee before anything else happens.

Mr. Rutherford takes my move the wrong way. He half-rises, reaches for my hands, clasps my left between both of his.

He says, "Try with me, dear. We can calm the waters. Let's call on our Heavenly Savior. I know you still want to find Him, deep down—"

I jerk my hand away. It's urgent I get out of there.

Bobby is on the old man. I think he took my backing away for more than it was. Like I felt grabbed and needed defending. I really just had to go out and pee. But Bobby grips Mr. Rutherford's shirt front in one fist and shakes till the buttons pop.

"Can't you learn a fuckin' thing, you old fart? Who really needs forgivin' here?"

I slug Bobby on the arm as I'm heading to the side door. He lets go of the shirt.

Also, I yelled at him, *Chill out. Don't do nothin' crazy. I'm just stepping outside for one minute—* Things to that effect.

Okay, maybe it was not the best time for me to go out of there, but like I say—I couldn't figure a better way to handle things until I got a break.

Wind had slowed to a long deep sigh, blowing a fine billow of spray off the roof of the house. The air was at least 20 degrees cooler than in the afternoon, but with that unsettled feel, teetering between brisk and muggy. Where you're breathing water on every inhale. It felt like I tumbled down the steps, but I didn't actually fall. It was full dark, of course, but the low clouds reflected enough light to find my car. I got wet to the knees crossing the grass and gravel.

There were some napkins in the door pocket and a Red Bull on the floor of the backseat. I chugged about half of that and put it in the cupholder. Then I went round back of the tree and took care of business.

I zipped up my jacket and went back to the house. In all? I'd say I was outside about five-six minutes.

One of the chairs had fell over while I was outside. Bobby was standing, fists still balled up.

Mr. Rutherford was back on the couch. He appeared much the worse for wear. His shirt was ripped, and his face was wet. Like maybe he'd shed some tears. He looked to me, and I could see he was seriously scared now. He didn't say a word, but he was breathing pretty hard.

No, Bobby was not hitting him. Never did I see him do that. In fact, I know he didn't hit him because once I was back in the room, he said—"I can't rough up an old man no worse than that."

Bobby stepped farther back from the couch, punched his palm with his opposite hand. I wouldn't say he was actively menacing Mr. Rutherford at that point.

But no doubt Mr. Rutherford felt menaced anyways.

Bobby looks at me and says, "It's up to you, LaDene."

His knife is on the table. It's open, full-length. I hadn't seen when that happened. He picks it up. It points up from his hand.

The old man cringes. I think he whimpered a little.

I say, "What in the hell?"

Bobby backs me toward the door. He's got a hand on my shoulder and he kind of shoves me to the wall by the door. I can see his eyes flash from all the substances he's got on board. I know he's messed up, and I want to keep him calm. So much as possible.

Yes, I felt worried.

Bobby talks like he thinks he's telling me a big secret. Like Mr. Rutherford won't hear. I don't remember exactly. His words got mixed up in my head, things like—

It's gettin' real now, girl. Shit does get real. You know you need to step up. Git it off your chest. Kick it outta your head. Stand up f'yerself. For me. You can do it. Fight back for once—

He grips my arm hard, gives me a little shake. I know he wants to rile me up. Wants me to share his feeling. His purpose, such as it is.

Well, yeah. I knew he might hurt me. Like by accident, he might.

Then he said, "I'll be right out here. You do what needs doin'."

He pushes the door, lets it hang open. I hear him clomp down the steps. Cold air flows into the room.

I'm holding the knife. I see it in my hand, but honest to God, I didn't notice how it got there. Guess I was too focused on Bobby pushing me to the wall. He must of gave it to me before he went down the steps. I can hear him shuffling around just outside. I feel like he's listening for whatever I'm going to do.

Mr. Rutherford gives me that look of misery. He takes another shot at talking.

Almost breathless, he says, "I don't know what this is about. What does he want from me? Do I need to admit I've made mistakes? Sure, I've made mistakes! I did my best, but in 38 years on the job, you're bound to make a few. I'm sorry if people got hurt. I'm sorry if you and your cousin got hurt. But you've got to understand, your cousin is a dangerous man. He's committed crimes here. You've got to help me. I know you didn't want this, but you'll be deemed an accessory—"

Sh-sh-sh-shoosh. I tell him, "Now's not such a good time to carry on like that."

But he keeps it up.

"You don't want to get in any deeper here. I know you don't. You've been through some hard knocks, but I can see you're not a bad person. Your cousin is dangerous. He's high on drugs. You've got to get us out of here—"

It seemed like he was afraid to get up from the couch. Maybe Bobby told him not to. But he'd moved right to the edge of it and waved his hands at me.

Was I angry at him? Not really. I didn't blame him for any-thing. But his talk was getting irritating. He thought he had to persuade me of shit I already knew, and he wouldn't let up. What if Bobby could hear him going on and on? The door was wide open. He might barrel back in any minute. Yell at me, get more irate. Gods knows what.

I said it in a harder tone, "Just shush, now. Quit talking." I raised the knife. I had it pointed down, not like knife-fighting. More like you would open up a pumpkin. I know that much.

But it got his attention.

"Come down on the floor here," I told him. Motioned to the area right in front of the couch. He did like I said, kind of slid down. I knelt down to him.

I bend in close and whisper, "I'm going to hurt you just one tiny bit. Not bad. Just for show. So my cousin lays off—"

He stares at the knife and his face twists up. Tears flood his eyes. He starts talking again, all the same stuff, in be-tween whimpering— *You don't want to do this—Don't do this—Don't be a criminal—You'll regret it— I've got children, grandchildren, a family—*

Maybe he didn't believe I was trying to help in the best way I could figure. Which kind of makes me mad. I press him back to the skirt of the couch and cut him right along his hairline. A little slice on each side, above both eyebrows. That can put out a show of blood real fast. And it did—blood runs down his face.

A crazy feeling floods over me—I am making him bleed. The room starts to throb and my ears are ringing. But the old man finally quits talking. I hear his breath, coming harder than ever.

I also cut him on his chest, along his collarbone. About a two-inch slice. Just to get some red on his shirt, where it would show. There wasn't enough. So I did it again on the other side.

You see, it had to look real.

All that while, he's fighting me in a sad, pathetic way— slapping at me with his fingers, open hands. Trying to scoot away along the floor. It was from fright, I think. Not from pain. What I did couldn't of hurt him that bad.

Of course, it made me feel awful. I didn't want him going through this. Any of this.

My mind hates to picture it.

I beg him again, "Pretend like you're dying. Just pretend. Play possum." Make my voice kind of harsh, to convince him. When he keeps whimpering, I finally put the tip of the knife right under his chin. I say it louder, "Do not talk. Act like you're dying."

He did start to gasp. I think that was his way of playing dead.

Could Bobby hear from outside? I could see the red of his cigarette just below the steps, moving around, like he's pacing back and forth. He had put a shit ton of expectations on me, and all in that moment, it sent a shot of madness into my heart. Anger, I mean—it burned into me from that cigarette glow.

So I take the knife in my two hands. Reared up on my knees, over the couch seat, and I wail on that end cushion. Stab it and slash it to shreds. Up and again and again. The stuffing puffs out in hunks and bits. I'm sucking air, maybe I'm grunting. Probably I said some shit. Maybe I yelled—*Quiet, dammit, shut yer goddam mouth, there, there, there, there. Now, yer done? Done with the talkin'? Shut it and keep it that way—*

I don't know what all I may of said.

No idea how long it took. Soon enough, Bobby came back inside.

I was sitting on the floor. It felt like a little time had passed. At last the old man was quiet. He looked bloodied enough. But I know he didn't lose a lot of blood. Not from those tiny cuts I made.

Bobby's eyes got wide as saucers.

He didn't smile per say. But he sounded satisfied.

Okay, he sounded glad in a way.

"You did it, Baby Girl. Did it for both of us. I knew you had it in you. You're my real true sweetheart!"

I put a hand on the end of the couch and rassle up to my feet. I see the knife is still there, buried in the stuffing.

"Let's go," I say.

Bobby is eyeing the old man. "We can't leave him like that," he says. "He's sputtering—"

It's true. Mr. Rutherford was wheezing, like, but he was mostly keeping still, and it seems like he had his eyes closed at that point. He was an awful sight. I admit that much. But I knew he would come through okay. Nothing so horrific had happened to him.

Bobby reached for the couch cushion, one that was intact. Like he thought he should smother the man. End his suffering. So I picked up the knife.

"Leave it!" I said. "Move! Let's go!" I swiped the blade toward the door, took the camp lantern by its handle, and headed out. I heard the cushion hit the floor behind me, and Bobby came along. We left the old man in the dark.

Well, I knew he might be a little shaky. I didn't want him knocking the lamp over and getting burned, now, did I?

The keys were in my pocket. I turned out the lantern and got in the driver's seat. Bobby got in beside me. His knee was bouncing up and down at a furious pace, and he drummed on his knees, hummed some little musical noises. I wondered if he might be ready to crash.

We wheeled out of there, back down Duck Creek Road, Highway 83, onto the Interstate. The roads were wet, and spray flew up around us. I was careful not to drive fast. I don't make a habit of driving drunk, but I know how to be careful when I might not be perfectly legal.

South—that was my only thought. The stateline. The Interstate bridge, West Virginia, pulled off in Parkersburg. Took the main drag a couple miles south and stopped at a Qwik Mart. Bobby went inside to buy some stuff for the drive.

I got my purse from the backseat, found my phone. It was there the whole time. Yes, it was. In the ladies room, I took care of myself, cleaned up a bit. Then I called my sister Effie. I thought she'd be the most helpful. Ask the least questions. And she lives close, on the north side of Devola. Thank God, she picked up right away.

It went more or less like this —

Ef, you remember Gramma Dot's house? You know where it is?

Course I know where it is.

I need you to drive out there. Take a flashlight. It's a real emergency. Somebody needs help.

You're not there yerself?

I need to be somewhere else. I'm helping somebody else.
Go right away. Go now. Please—

And she said, Okay—she'd go. That was all.

She did go, right? She found the old man and took care of him?

Yeah, yeah, right. You ask the questions. Anyways, that's the first thing I did was call Effie. Then I called home. My momma.

She didn't pick up right away, and when she did answer—about five rings in—her voice sounded sleepy and surprised at the same time. I didn't tell her anything about what had happened, didn't say where I was calling from. She knew something was wrong, though, because I never call them at night.

Her and Dad were already in bed, watching TV. There was Judge Judy or some such yammering in the background. Homey noise. I didn't say much. Told her I wouldn't be able to stop out on Sunday. Said I was sorry for that. Said I loved her and I loved Daddy. Just wanted to hear her voice.

Finally, she said, "If you're not going to tell me what's going on, then just be careful—" And that was that. We said good-bye.

It's not like I thought me and Bobby could escape consequences. We weren't trying to do that. Yes, I ditched my phone. Yes, I drove into West Virginia, found us a room, little mom-and-pop place, and parked my car in back. But it's not like I was trying to get to the Gulf and hop a boat somewhere you'd never find us. I only wanted a little time. A day. So we could get some rest. Maybe Bobby could come to his right mind, get in a little better shape to deal. Maybe we could talk in a serious vein, figure out what might be best for him, with his record and all.

He is family, and he was good to me coming up, like I said. Beyond that, I can't explain why I wound up with him, wanting to help him. It's like I could see his leg caught in an iron trap, so to say, and maybe I could pry him loose just enough so he could slip out? No, I was not beholden to him. Just wanted to stay on his good side, let him know I stood by him, and hope something better than what we did might come of it.

I made sure he drank water, ate a sandwich. In the motel, we snuggled on the bed. I left a gap open between the drapes to keep in touch with the world outside—wet leaves, security light shining down on the pavement. I could tell Bobby was about to crash. Every time he tried to talk, his voice went into slo-mo. Wide open spaces between the words, almost a slur. I kept my arms around him, held my cheek against his forehead.

He muttered about old times at Gramma's house, what our parents might think if the two of us showed up together sometime, what we might do for money in some imaginary future he was playing inside his head. Random shit all over again.

A little house—a little family—sweet times.

Once or twice he asked, "Don't you really feel better—got that old shit—off your chest?"

Even now, I can't begin to answer that.

The last thing he said was something like, "So—do you think—we can make it in the morning?"

For a second I thought he meant, might we manage to have sex after all this time?

But I asked him, "Make it where? Where do you think we can go?"

It sounded like he said, "Somewhere," or maybe it was, "Some way."

I knew he was passed out at that point, but I answered anyway, "You know there's not a place on earth we can run to. No way we're not in deep shit. Best thing, I figure, is if we stay put and soak up the little peace we can in whatever time we've got."

Next thing I knew, the gap between the drapes was bright with sun and your bunch was pounding down the door. So that's how I come to find myself in this cramped little room with y'all.

Enjoy more about
I Never Do This
Meet the Author
Check out author appearances
Explore special features

ANESA MILLER is a native of Wichita, Kansas, a graduate of the University of Idaho, a long-term resident of Ohio, and recipient of an Ohio Arts Council Fellowship for creative writing. Her fiction, essays, and poetry have appeared widely, and her previous novel, *Our Orbit,* was a finalist in regional fiction in the Next Generation Indie Book Awards.

Acknowledgements

As the author of *I Never Do This*, I wish to thank those who, directly and obliquely, have enabled the book's writing and publication: The residents of lovely Marietta, Ohio, and its environs; my teachers, including but not limited to Nancy Zafris, Pat Schneider, Patricia Lewis, Bob Wrigley, Mary Clearman Blew, Kim Barnes, Joy Passanante, and Daniel Orozco; all of those who encouraged me by reading and reviewing my previous novel, *Our Orbit*; and, of course, the remarkable crew at Sibylline Press. Special thanks to all of my supportive friends and family, among whom the late Jaak Panksepp must have particular mention for making so many things possible.

Book Club Questions

1. What is your impression of LaDene Faye Howell? Does your impression change over the course of her story? Do you trust her to "tell all in full truth and hold nothing back?"

2. What do you think of LaDene's parents' plans for her life after her time at the New Dawn Ministry?

3. How would you describe LaDene's relationship with her parents? Is it surprising that she stays close to them after she finishes school and moves out of their home?

4. Describe LaDene's relationships with her sisters and with the girls she meets at the Ministry.

5. Who does Bobby Frank blame for his problems? What is his role in LaDene's life? What do you make of their feelings for each other?

6. As a school principal, Mr. Rutherford claims that he informed parents about "teen bootcamps" to help them get control of children with severe behavioral problems, "as a last resort." What would you say to parents considering this option?

7. What do you make of LaDene's decision to choose adoptive parents for her baby? Do you think she makes a good decision?

8. LaDene says she loved her newborn baby but also that she would have been better off getting an abortion. What do you think of these claims?

9. How would you describe LaDene's life as an adult living on her own? Does she need to change her habits? What would it take for her to do this?

10. Do you see any future for LaDene and Bobby Frank's relationship?

Sibylline Press is proud to publish the brilliant work of women authors over 50. We are a woman-owned publishing company and, like our authors, represent women of a certain age.

Rottenkid: A Succulent Story of Survival
BY BRIGIT BINNS

Pub Date: 3/5/24
ISBN: 9781960573995
Memoir, Trade paper, $19, 320 pages

Prolific cookbook author Brigit Binns' coming-of-age memoir—co-starring her alcoholic actor father Edward Binns and glamorous but viciously smart narcissistic mother—reveals how simultaneous privilege and profound neglect led Brigit to seek comfort in the kitchen, eventually allowing her to find some sense of self-worth. A memoir sauteed in Hollywood stories, world travel, and always, the need to belong.

1666: A Novel
BY LORA CHILTON

Pub Date: 4/2/24
ISBN: 9781960573957
Fiction, Trade paper, $17, 224 pages

The survival story of the Patawomeck Tribe of Virginia has been remembered within the tribe for generations, but the massacre of Patawomeck men and the enslavement of women and children by land hungry colonists in 1666 has been mostly unknown outside of the tribe until now. Author Lora Chilton, a member of the tribe through the lineage of her father, has created this powerful fictional retelling of the survival of the tribe through the lives of three women.

I Never Do This: A Novel
BY ANESA MILLER

Pub Date: 4/16/24
ISBN: 9781960573988
Fiction, Trade paper, $17, 216 pages

This gothic novel presents the unforgetta-
ble voice of a young woman, LaDene Faye
Howell, who finds herself in police custody
recounting her story after her paroled cousin
Bobbie Frank appears and engages her in a
crime spree in the small town of Devola, Ohio.

The Goldie Standard: A Novel
BY SIMI MONHEIT

Pub Date: 5/7/24
ISBN: 9781960573971
Fiction, Trade paper, $19, 328 pages

Hilarious and surprising, this unapologetical-
ly Jewish story delivers a present-day take on a
highly creative grandmother in an old folks' home
trying to find her Ph.D granddaughter a husband
who is a doctor—with a yarmulke, of course.

Bitterroot: A Novel
BY SUZY VITELLO

Pub Date: 5/21/24
ISBN: 9781960573964
Fiction, Trade paper, 18, 296 pages

A forensic artist already reeling from the surprise death of her husband must confront the
MAGA politics, racism and violence raging in
her small town in the Bitterroot Mountains
of Idaho when her gay brother is shot and she
becomes a target herself.

For more books from **Sibylline Press**,
please visit our website at **sibyllinepress.com**

Printed in the USA
CPSIA information can be obtained
at www.ICGtesting.com
JSHW022311080324
58883JS00004B/4